The Lyons of Rabbit

Darby Guise

Bear Skin Bob Press

Also by Darby Guise

An American Beelzebub

The Drunk'unn Boat

Harmony in Bad Taste

The Lyons *of* Rabbit

The
Lyons of
Rabbit

A rabbit's foot may bring good luck to you, but it
brought none to the rabbit.
—Ambrose Bierce, *A Cynic Looks at Life*

1

His crew cut was strange, asymmetrical, different from the others. And if God had taught him anything, it was that it was more or less okay to be a prick. Fairness was key; firmness was negotiable (or perhaps it was the other way around).

He lived in the warren with the other rabbits. They seldom lived longer than four years nowadays, and he was approaching that grim benchmark; death seemed imminent. He put on his grey suit and exited his apartment with its metallic red door. He waved to his neighbor Jim in the lobby, and Jim fumbled a wave back; his splenic flexure emitted a sharp pain, contorting his torso into a spastic greeting. He clenched his teeth, smiling with awkward distress.

2

Tom got into his car and drove along the grove. The redwoods capitulated to the roadways working within their inner sanctum. Anfractuous, curious asphalt lanes. The rabbits pushed through the land in their tiny automobiles. Tom spotted George hopping along, sputtering woodchips this way and that as puffs of underbrush blew upward in his wake. Tom honked his horn, and George flicked up a quick hand as he busied himself towards whatever goal taunted him towards her. "Beautiful day, isn't it?" said Tom. He often spoke to himself during his drive to work. He encouraged an amicable self-talk along his twisty morning journey. He sipped coffee and yammered on with quick asides. The sun broke through in patches; much of the dew had evaporated.

3

There was a lot of affinity between the terrorist and the writer, thought Bill. And he hoped that his end credits had music. The final tune, or the sum total of the entirety of his show plugged in and worked out, chord progressions and key changes, running along for three-ish minutes or less. *Would it be in a minor key?* A fetching falsetto? Would little clips and bloopers or post-credit denouements play alongside the scrolling text? And who would be watching? Who was this imagined, veiled audience sitting quietly in the dark? The voyeurs solidifying his program, snacking away while tuned to his frequency. "I was here! *They* saw me!" He felt like yelling this at the world. In the past tense, no doubt—future Bill, no longer viewed, forgotten, stray seats with only six occupants. (*One gets up, a chubby man in overalls with thick, black-rimmed glasses. He walks away from the screen and down the hall, and the exit door budges open.*)

Bill parked his car beside a pale green Buick and walked towards his tree. He walked slowly (ambling was the word), and he climbed the makeshift ladder of wooden planks hammered into the tree's trunk. He gripped and stepped and pulled and got himself through the hatch and into his office. And voila! He closed the door and opened a window and sat on his couch and unburdened his lungs; he let out a long sigh, and he grabbed his horned typewriter and set to work. He looked up at the words on the wall. "Stay hungry. Stay foolish." Two *Stays* with three dots written in black Sharpie, an ode to his early days with the tree. Above them, "Make good," his new motto, his latest dictum. Subjective and uncertain. *Make good by what*? By *who*? He shrugs. "Just… make good." Simple and shrewd.

Bill had been a writer for exactly six weeks; before, he'd been a machinist (and one of the best of the warren). It was through his machining that he'd actually won his literary role. It started one night during a late-August storm. He'd been tinkering with it for quite some time. He'd seen it in his mind's eye, three-dimensional, a spinning holograph, de facto TV (pixels with heft and girth); he'd projected that image into the world, one small morsel at a time. Chunk by chunk. He'd taken the material from his own flesh, pound for pound. Bite for bite—he'd spit it at *It* and hoped the larger whole would accept each new morsel, absorb it, put it to use in its gelatinous core. It moaned and burped and quivered.

It ate.

It had eaten a lot. It had required a lot. It was a newborn in need of nurturing, love, harmony, gentleness. And Bill had provided this, in spades, no doubt, and now the machine had matured; it had sprouted a series of metallic quills and scissor-like spikes and ingrown toenails. A death trap to the uninitiated, but a series of levers and pulleys to the trained, masochistic eye. A machine of incalculable beauty, alloyed to perfection. He pressed the keys, and the gears went to work.

13

4

Pam smiled at the child seated across from her. Its fur on end—large, fearful eyes. The room was blasé, sanitized, checkered green floors and walls of light taupe. It had seen this two-chair setup many times. The boy sat still, feet dangling, eyes downward. Pam could hear a faint humming coming from his lips, a mnemonic recording, a song played not so much for comfort as habit. Melodies from the traumatized mind... *blurred white noise*. Their chairs faced each other, separated by a few feet; Pam hunched over and touched his knee.

"You're a brave boy, you know that?"

He didn't seem to acknowledge her words; he kept humming; his feet started to swing.

"Do you remember what it looked like? What color it was?"

The young rabbit shook his head.

"That's alright, hon. Can I get you anything? Are you hungry?"

The melody shifted. The song took a hairpin turn, mutating in a parade of new notes; its beat quickened, then slowed. It stopped; he looked up.

"It said that... *It* said it was hungry... '*Sooo verrryy hungry.*'" His voice morphed, echoes of the creature came to the fore, an air of coolness and rabidness. "Kept saying that—over and over."

"It's okay, hon. You're safe now."

Pam walked the halls, and Lynne emerged from a side door and kept pace.

"Hi, beautiful. How's your mornin'?"

Lynne nudged up beside her, her fur bristling against Pam's arm.

"I got another one today. Poor kid... his whole family gone: mom, dad, brothers... sisters."

"What was it this time?"

"He couldn't say, but it sounded a lot like Jack."

Lynne stopped and unconsciously gripped Pam's arm—shocked, excited. *Time's up*, she thinks; she tightens her hold around Pam's sleeve. "Wow, how long has it been since we've had a Jack in our forest?"

"Ages, but nothing's for certain yet."

"But?"

"But... I got a feeling *he's* here again."

Jean sat at her desk, her door open. Small framed paintings of lizards and mice tacked to the wall, to the left, an overly large clock with cartoon hands. Pam appeared in the doorframe.

"Hi, Jean."

"Hey, Pam. What can I do for you?"

"I just had a talk with Tim Dominguez. You know the boy?"

"I heard some of what happened. His whole family up on Route 36, wasn't it?"

"Yeah, bad one. Listen, I think I should probably go out there."

"You think that's necessary?"

"Yes, from what the boy told me, it sounded a lot like Jack."

"*Jack*?"

"Yeah."

"You know, we haven't had one of those since—"

"Since the Bufords back in '85. But the signs... I'm telling ya. We should have a look."

"Okay, whatever you think. Take Hymen with you."

"Is he in?"

"Yeah, check his office, and when you get back, come fill me in. Okay?"

"Okay."

She knocked on Hymen's door. She could hear him bustling inside.

"Come in."

Pam entered. "How's ol' Hymie today?"

"Oh, tired as a tit. How's darling Pam?"

She tried to keep up the tone—joviality even in the face of a freshly arrived killer. Undermine the responsibility, turn up her nose at all the seriousness. "Glowing with springtime freshness and... a sneaking suspicion that we got a Jack on our hands."

"*Jack*?"

(And now for the dour turn...)

"That's right. And Jean wants me to go have a look, and lucky you, you get to come along."

"Oh, thank heavens," said Hymen. "I wouldn't want to miss a face-to-face encounter with a son-of-a-bitchin' Jack right about now, would I? Look at ol' Hymen, hasn't even had a sip of coffee or taken his mornin' shit, and here he is being carted off with the likes of you... to check out a Christly Jack no less. Goddamn blue Mondays, Pam. A goddamn cursed day."

"Stop your whining. I'll buy you breakfast on the way."

Hymen smiled, his humor unremitting, renewed by a dash of feminine optimism; what's a murdering lunatic to a rabbit who's suffered hemorrhoids and gallstones? Daily battles (the ongoing struggle) having eroded his causal claim to happy endings, anyway.

"Ah, a *calming* balm for this tiger's toothache," said Hymen.

"Two morning sliders... extra ketchup, medium coffee, apple fritter."

"Oh, music to Hymen's ears."

"Hymie heaven... Well, what are we waiting for? Upward and onward, my fat, furry friend. I'll grab my keys."

The rabbits got into Pam's car, and she lit a cigarette, and Hymen busied himself turning the radio dials. The voice of Pete van Everdynk sprang out of the car speakers.

"Be careful, folks. We got a tree down on Ash Lane due to last night's storm. Cleaning crews are on-site, and they'd like me to remind you to keep your speed below thirty. Eastbound traffic over on Highway 9 is moving, but further on..."

Hymen sat back and stared at the blur of trees.

"You know, I haven't heard of a Jack around here since—"

"The Bufords," said Pam.

"Yeah, that's right. The Bufords. Hell, this could really turn out to be one shitty Monday after all."

"Here's hoping," said Pam.

She pulled off the main road and circled around to the drive-thru at Patty's Diner.

"... the six bodies were discovered late yesterday evening. Eyewitnesses report that the bodies were found ravaged. Still no suspects in custody. Local sheriff John Huckston said that anyone with any information should call the hotline and warned against unnecessary risks. 'Travel in pairs, in a fluffle, or not at all.'"

5

Bill was humming. Somewhere along his morning maneuvers, he'd acquired the tune. Rogue bits of processed information that had somehow gone unnoticed, only to resurface with a vengeance further on down the line. It sounded like something from the university. A marching band's half-time promenade. Architecture and steeples and mouths—somehow, it had found its way in, and he drummed the table with his furry paws, recalling the beat.

He stared at his machine: his horned apparatus. Metal, antlers, an unstructured mess; he hit the *e* key and watched the type hammer swing. He wrote, "Dating her was a series of blowjobs and missed calls." He sat back... then he wrote, "He thought of himself as a painful vat of water." He figured that was enough for the day; the bell had been rung, and he packed up his things and left.

He wondered if writing was nothing but a game—Snakes and Ladders consumed by moralists struggling with copyright issues. Then he saw a tree shake, and an immense figure dropped down from the foliage.

It was *brilliant*—a rogue queen. A goddamn human. The outlaw among the outlaws. She fell gracefully, landing smack in front of Bill. She eyed him beneath her cap as Bill halted, paralyzed—damn near dropped his typewriter. He blinked, pooped a small pellet. *Where had she come from...?*

6

Long ago, the squares had done away with all their freaks. Assimilating them was easier than expelling them; they had concluded this (a genius idea!); they processed them into their center. Only a few wished to remain anonymous, live outside the rules of strict labels. The world of men had yelled at everyone, "Be someone, anyone, but be something... invent, re-create, re-label. Mix and match and ad-lib. But fill out your form; fill it in with biographical banners, labels, and anti-labels—innovate, repurpose, and amalgamate: *give it a name.* Breathe life into this uniformity, this *ghastly* sameness. Let us give you what you want. Let us swallow you up and adopt you... let us adapt to you. Let us learn how to overcome you. Just give us your definition. What are *you* called? What do *you* do?"

7

Pam stepped out of the car with Hymen, and they trudged up the slope between the trees. There was ample room for them to move, and the sun was shining, and it seemed like an altogether peaceful day, and then she saw the breaks in the branches—ahead, the scene of the crime.

The bodies had been taken away, but bits of fur and blood clung to the earth, insects scavenged the remains of organs and debris and created a groundswell of activity. Pam looked at the dirt and then moved her gaze upward, taking in the scene as best she could.

"What a fucking mess," said Hymen.

"What is it the cowboys used to say? '*Or it'll do till the mess gets here.*'"

"Sounds about right," said Hymen, "and you think it's Jack?"

"Looks that way."

"Certainly does," agreed Hymen. "Fuck."

8

Bill tried to stammer some words, expel his excitement... or, better yet, his shock. He had mistaken it. He thought it was a girl; its grace feminine, powerful, light, and elegant—but, when he looked closer, he noticed its face: features rose to the fore, and a man's drawl rang out; its mustache moved unevenly above its lip.

"Howdy, little thing. The name's Doc. Who the fuck are you?"

"B-B-Bill," said Bill.

"Okay, Bill, I'm in a bit of a jam. How about helping a partner out, okay? Whatdya say?"

Bill nodded, his eyes fixed on the towering slender man before him, dressed in a long black coat and a wide-brimmed cowboy hat and pleated pants. When he moved, he appeared to float. An ease and elegance accompanied him... yet there was something sinister (even dangerous) about him; Bill could sense this, sniff it out amongst the man's defining attributes. *Don't fuck with this asshole,* thought Bill.

It started to rain, and somewhere... under some tree... some rabbit wondered how many cellphones would get murdered that night.

Bill stood up and straightened himself out. A smidge of courage had resurfaced in his being; he saw his predicament for what it was. Help Doc... or risk running afoul of this creature—oozing mystery... unease?

"What can I do for you?" asked Bill.

"Well, let's start by taking care of these."

He showed Bill his shackled hands, and Bill nodded (he knew what to do); he gestured at the creature to follow him. They made their way through the woods; the rain picked up, and to the south, they heard a woodpecker beating the hell out of some tree.

As they walked, Doc told Bill about his last few days, living hand to mouth, feeding on the animals and the land. He told him about snaring a raccoon and skinnin' it and guttin' it and roastin' it atop a fire—he said it was delicious, and then he said, "In the jungle, stupidity counts as consent... the Venus flytrap taught me that."

Bill hopped along, and Doc followed gingerly. He was quite a bit taller than Bill, ducking and bobbing his way among the branches. Bill was taking him to his workshop, an underground space teeming with tools. Surely a bit of welding along with some finicky and precise mucking about with pins and chisels would release Doc, unlock his chains. And as they walked, Doc spoke of his adventures; he told Bill about falling for some young damsel whose husband had been a highfalutin asshole employed by the royal court. He (Doc) had been a regular nobody, a ronin, wandering from town to town, toting gun and knife—a pest, really... except the young damsel had seen something in him, something desirable (the glimmer in his eye, his genital outline), and the two had begun a heated affair. And then (somehow... someway...) the husband had discovered their liaison, and Doc was set up, imprisoned, a false charge; he was expected to be hanged... but due to a strange series of events the morning of his scheduled execution, he'd escaped (a fire, a mad arsonist, a blaze in the castle's westward sector). Doc had been left alone, just him and the hangman; all the others had rushed off, halting the proceedings. He took his chance, kicked the bastard in the testes, snagged his hat, and ran (still shackled) and scurried off into the bush. He'd been living in the woods ever since (for over a week, he supposed), and then he'd met Bill, and that about summed up his relatively clichéd adventure.

They arrived, and Bill unlatched the wooden door lying flush with the ground; he swung it open and bade Doc to come inside. The cowboy took off his hat and entered Bill's factory. He descended the steps and made his way down into the earth.

$$9$$

Hymen touched the branch; it had been snapped during the fracas with the Dominguez family. When he pulled his paw away, there was a bit of coagulated blood on it. He looked over at Pam as she examined the scene, her eyes thoughtful and concentrated, trying hard to make sense of it all, how it'd all played out. She eyed the ground, sniffed with her little rabbit nose, unbuttoned her coat pocket and snapped some photos. Hymen sipped his coffee and quietly burped. He thought Pam was beautiful. And he, the old-timer, lit a cigarette and observed his partner, the lovely young mother and wife... the shrewd detective... the imaginative babe.

"Hymen, come here."

He walked over to her, and she pointed to the ground.

"What does that look like to you?"

"Hmm..."

Hymen bent low and touched the viscous liquid, silver and white and swirling black. It had pooled along in a narrow groove by a canopying linden tree. It was sticky. He pulled his fingers apart, and the liquid tightened, then relaxed, and then tightened again. "What the hell?" He sniffed at it and then wiped the residue on his pants. "What is it?"

Pam shook her head. "I'm not sure. Strange though, right?"

"Yeah... strange about covers it."

They turned and looked at the space anew, slowly spinning and trying to understand, and then they saw it... sprinting at them. A black blur... wild fur... ivory chompers...

A fierce cry.

Pam screamed.

Hymen fell over.

The beast snatched Hymen up in its jaws. Their mass (prey plus predator) shook the earth; it galloped past.

Pam swung around, trying hard to follow the action with her eyes. She could hear the snapping of branches, Hymen shrieking, stabbed by teeth (enamel, dentin, cementum, and pulp), and then it all died down... or Pam's hearing went out, extinguished—she ran towards the car. Her deaf-mute mind frozen, only a single thought, "Don't look back," focus ahead, get to safety, get to structure, get away.

Run!

10

Doc picked up a small clump of greasy gears and wiped his fingers on the cloth on Bill's worktable. It was a large, open bunker; even for someone Doc's size, the space accommodated him easily. He sat and watched Bill grab his welding kit and ignite the torch; he cut the chain, then onto the picks, slotting them in and out, at this angle and that, and, eventually, the manacles opened—Doc was freed. He rubbed his wrists, swollen red with irritation.

"Quite a place you got here, Bill."

Bill smiled. "A home away from home."

The fluorescent lights flickered above them. Walls lined with tools and workbenches strewn with parts, semi-completed projects, Doc thought he saw an astrolabe among the mess. A TV was ripped apart, and the skeleton of an old automobile lay at the far end of the rectangular hall. *A factory indeed*, thought Doc. He turned and walked slowly among the pieces, eyeing the machines and the parts as Bill put his chisels away.

"Are you hungry?" asked Bill.

"Famished."

Bill snapped his fingers, and Doc sat on a stool; he watched as his host disappeared through a side door. He heard a beep, then a whistle, and soon Bill reemerged holding a bowl of steaming stew. He plopped it in front of Doc, and Doc nodded to the rabbit.

"You've been a big help, Bill. Thank you." He took a mouthful—rich and spicy with a hint of sweetness. Roughly chopped herbs floated among the oily remains. "Oh, you succulent braised meat! Oh, you flavorsome veggies!" Doc had to restrain himself from the frenzy of tipping the bowl back and inhaling the stew in one swift go.

"Good?"

"Delicious." He continued to consume, spoonful after spoonful. "So, what is it you do around here?"

"Lots of tinkering, mostly. I was a machinist. Nowadays, though, ahem... I'm generally considered a writer... more or less."

Doc smiled. "A writer, eh? Good for you, Bill."

Doc knew from the tales he'd heard circulating the dust-covered towns and eked out from the mouths of emaciated vagabonds that each warren contained a supposed writer. Like a medicine man or chemist or prophet all rolled into one, they were in charge of conversing with the gods, an intermediary crafting the saga that would govern and guide their lot, separate it, maneuver it in *new* and wise and just directions. The storytellers interpreting God's plan, splicing the ingredients—the butchered raw word (heated and cooked and coiled), pathways and flavors edging the rabbit consciousness towards strange horizons (or perspectives? or maybe even abysses?).

Doc figured they were mostly full of shit.

"What are you writing now?"

"Hmm," he didn't usually talk about this (his process, his progress, his stories); he paused, and then he met Doc's gaze; he saw anticipation and remnants of stew on his face. *What the hell.* "Well, it's a story about the devil, actually. Well, maybe not the devil, exactly, but it could be. It's about a stranger who wanders into this town... is he the devil? A conman? Prophet? Saint? No one knows for sure, and weird events start cropping up among the townsfolk, shifting what was once routine and comfortable and safe into a dangerous game—addicting to some, terrifying to others, but growing and shifting and expanding constantly... consuming their focus, their sanity, their..."

11

Heart.

It was pounding, broken up in quick, painful palpitations. Her lungs heaved, and through the downpour, she looked out. She could see the beast. It was eating... eating Hymen. He was in pieces now. The beast was still too far for her to make out any of the gory details. She was locked in her automobile. Somewhere among the ruins of Hymen's body parts—among the undergrowth and weeds and dirt—were her keys. In the rush to escape, they must have fallen out. She sat back and watched the beast; it shoved a piece of Hymen's hind leg, nudging it with its nose. She grabbed her cellphone and dialed Jean's number; it went straight to voicemail.

"Howdy-ho. This is Jean Pomagrowski. Please leave me a message after the beep, and I'll try and get back to you..."

Pam kept her eyes on the beast; it was still eating, but its ferocity had slowed; now, it sniffed and pushed portions of Hymen around, taking bites here and there, casually pulling him apart, separating meat from bone, musculature from tendon. *What kind of fucking Jack is this?* thought Pam. Something she hadn't yet seen or guessed could even exist. An opponent seemingly arising out of nowhere, a demon stalking their *goddamn* forest.

"Poor fucking Hymen," she said, "that poor fucking geezer."

Pam looked at the crumpled-up bag of fast food on the passenger-side floor, greasy patches among its base. Hymen's last meal. Now that very same meal was in Jack—eaten by eating Hymen. The beast let out a long growl, and Pam's eyes darted up as she watched Jack approach the car.

12

Jim was at home with the kids. Mandy was on the floor yelling; Sandra had stolen her toy (a doll with raggedy, thick-knit red hair). Jim had them both stand before him; he passed sentence, had Sandra apologize to Mandy. A slightly ashamed (but still pissed off) Sandra offered the doll back—her pouty, childish look aimed at the hardwood floor.

"Go ahead, Mandy. Sandra's sorry. You won't do it again, will you, young lady?"

Sandra kept her gaze low and shook her head, submissive to her father's rules of polite, playful conduct. No grabbing, no stealing, no biting, pulling hair, or pushing.

The phone rang.

"Play nice now, girls."

Sandra nodded, and Mandy said, "Yes, Daddy."

Jim walked across the apartment towards the kitchen and grabbed the phone from the wall.

"Hello."

"Jim! I need you... I'm stuck in the car. There's a fucking..."

13

Jack felt good. He felt full; the carnage was fun. In a low, husky breath, he let out his catchphrase. *"So verrryy hungry."* He mouthed it, the words coming out in an almost inaudible hum. He had just devoured another rabbit; the other had sprung back into her cage, eyeing him fearfully through the glass windows. He breathed up against it. Rain soaked his coat; he ran his tongue across his teeth, scraping the grooves and loosening any bits of stray meat. He licked the window, and then he pushed his head against the car, feeling its weight, its mass. It was heavier than he'd expected. Jack watched the terrified rabbit inside; she was speaking into a phone, eyes fixed on him. Jack burped and sat down lazily; he closed his eyes, mouthed the words: *"So verrryy hungry..."* His drawl turning into a yawn. His breath slowed. He was whisked off into dreams, a carnivore's coma, his innards working hard to break down Hymen—converting the old rabbit into premium fuel.

Pam sat smoking; Jack lay only a few feet away from the driver-side door. She hoped desperately that Jim would hurry. She watched Jack's ribcage expand and compress, up and down.

14

Jim was coming to the rescue... well, sort of. Pam had the car; he had one of the neighbors (Ms. Kenduska) watch the kids; he was using the underground route, a series of tunnels connecting the town. It would take him longer than driving, but if he got started *tout de suite*, he might be able to make it there in time. *God*, he thought, *please let me get there in time.* He hopped along the circular tunnels. Lights fitted into the dirt illuminated the brown-black earth and gave an orange glow to the route. He barely saw anyone; he hopped, paying attention to the upcoming intersections, left then right... straight ahead... go, go, go.

He took a sharp left turn and skidded out along the earth; he caught his balance and thought about Sandra and Mandy. The shock and pain that would surely follow—unless he hurried... unless he could somehow save their mother... save his wife. A pain had developed in his chest, but he kept up his speed. Worry and fear propelled him onward; he dug deep and kept on. Soon, he would be there. Soon, he could help...

or, at the very least, *try*. Why hadn't he brought any weapons? His gosh darn gun? What would he do when he saw this Jack figure? He supposed most questions would be answered shortly, no point fretting, *run, run, run*.

He thought of their courtship as he neared his destination. The first time he'd laid eyes on her. Beautiful Pam, all dolled up—always prim, always proper. He wasn't the only one after her hand. Derek Hampton had fancied her too—and Tom Wellington as well. But somehow, she had chosen him, and this meant the world to him. Colored him as desirable, something he hadn't been typically thought of as. She had elevated him among the warren through the simple act of selection. He knew she probably wondered about the others, daydreamed about potential lives, constructed fictionalized accounts (Mrs. Pam Wellington wearing a silk camel-colored dress with her dashing husband, Tom, and his pompadour-style coif). But she had chosen him among all the others, and now he was hurrying to her defense, to her aid, to her salvation... he neared the spot, and the tunnel turned upward. He took it, pushed his head out; it popped out in the rain. He could see her car about a hundred yards off, and beside it, the beast, Jack. *Was it sleeping?* He moved slowly; he would loop around and get her out. Thunder crashed, and Jim maneuvered towards the car, all the while keeping his eyes fixed on the slumbering beast.

15

Doc was fascinated. Bill had just summed up in broad strokes his newest machine. It looked like a weapon, like a metal glove one wore, spikes sliding in and out as the individual tightened and loosened their fist. *This could pack quite a wallop*, thought Doc—but Bill told him that it was actually a key to a certain box, requiring the wearer to insert their arm, shoulder deep in a dank, dark hole... then clench and rotate. If the key didn't fit (an intruder alert!), a blade would shoot down and sever the wrist in one swift go.

"Brutal."

Doc looked up; a fly (in the midst of being devoured) eyed him from the far corner in its kaleidoscopic vision.

"Yeah, I made it for an elderly rabbit"—the spider took another bite—"a *real crazy* bitch... she's trying to protect her more personal assets from intruders... and family, I guess. She came up with the idea. A mini Reign of Terror, a private French Revolution. Works like a charm, too."

Doc smiled as he watched Bill tinker and toy among his designs. He rubbed his face vigorously. "Say, Bill, you ever heard of Purson's bear?"

He shook his head. "No, I don't think so. What is it?"

"Oh, nothing..."—the fly was still alive (halfway eaten, halfway gone); Doc's mouth made a kind of twisting or smacking sound—"anyway, my mind's a little all over the place. Thanks again for the help, eh, Big Bill."

Bill smiled; he still, in fact, didn't trust Doc, but he felt compelled to help him, offer him things (accommodations, food, stories) even though he still hadn't shaken off the notion that Doc wasn't entirely the benevolent stranger he purported to be. He was kind and lithe, but not without a sinister undercurrent propelling him, guiding him.

Doc smiled, and Bill, in an uncharacteristic gesture (a clumsy burst of movement), knocked over the metal glove. He tried to catch it, and the end sliced his finger, and he recoiled, and the glove fell and landed on his leg, puncturing his hindquarter. He gasped, his eyes wide with pain and disbelief.

"Oh my God... Oh my God," repeated Bill.

The glove was impaled in his leg. Blood rushed and colored his light-brown fur.

"Fucking hell!" cried Bill.

Doc stood up; he calmly came over. He knelt beside the rabbit, put one hand on the metal glove. It stood erect, on end, a marker in the meat.

Bill squirmed on the ground as Doc readied to articulate his plan, to administer aid.

"I'm going to pull it out. Okay, Bill? Just relax now. On three. One... Two... Three..."

16

Jim watched Jack as he neared the car, carefully making his steps. Pam eyed him from the car's interior. She could feel her heart quicken, her blood pumping. "Please, God, let us get out of this." She said this to herself—she felt focused... hyper-focused; adrenaline was running wild, too *goddamn* much though, any more and she might tap out her reserves, then what? Would she pass out? And what a disaster that would be. Jim dragging her unconscious body... then Jack waking up, coming for them, eating them, mixing them up with Hymen and the Dominguezes and Patty's Diner's bouquet of eats 'n' drinks and whatever else lay in his ole gnarly gut. The rain kept up, and Jim neared the passenger-side door. He looked terrified, and she smiled at him through the window. She was so happy to see him. He gestured at her to hurry, open the door; she shuffled over and pulled the handle as lightly as she could. She burst into tears as Jim took her in his arms. She tried to muffle her sobs in the fur of his neck; he held her tight.

"It's okay, sweetheart. Let's get out of here, okay?"
Pam nodded, and Jim took her hand.
"Follow me, alright? And keep low."

17

Doc pulled it out (it made a squishing noise), and blood shot out, splattered against the side of the counter. Doc fetched a rod and a rubber belt from the nearest tabletop and fashioned a tourniquet around the rabbit's leg.

"It's not great, Big Bill. We may need to get you to a hospital."

"Let me see."

Bill cringed and looked; he unwound the rod (with shaky paws) and loosened the belt and eyed the wound; it was deep, but it wasn't gushing. Disinfecting it and stitching it up would probably do the trick.

"Hey, Doc."

"Yeah?"

"Fetch the alcohol over in the bathroom cabinet, would ya? There's some thread and a needle in there, too."

"You got it."

Doc walked to the back, easing his way through the workshop. A carefree spirit even amid this accidental bloodshed. Bill could hear him whistling as he rummaged around, looking for supplies.

"You find it?"

"Yes, sir." He wandered back, checking out the machines as he made his way towards the injured Bill, bleeding on the floor, squirming in pain. "Here you are, little buddy."

Bill grabbed the alcohol and doused his laceration. He grimaced and cursed the Lord. "*Ooooooo*, goddamn *mother-fucker* that hurts!"

Doc watched, standing above him. "What can I do, little buddy?"

Bill replied in nonsense, pain temporarily disabling his linguistic functions.

Doc flashed a smile, and Bill readied the thread and needle; he pressed his flapping flesh together and pierced the skin. He clenched his teeth and stiffened his back and pulled the thread through. He looked at his first successful pass; the skin clumped together. It reminded him of a cleft lip, and then he felt all woozy—a lightheaded haze was overtaking him. He looked up at Doc, who seemed to be grinning.

"You okay, Bill?"

But Bill was fading... it was too late; he flopped back, unconscious, still sporting a gaping hole in his leg, thread and needle at his side.

"Hmm..." said Doc.

18

Jack got up; he stretched and shook himself off. He eyed the vehicle; the little rabbit was gone. Sometime during his slumber, she must have run off. *So be it*, thought Jack. "*So verrryy hungry*," he said. He rolled in the dirt and coated himself in the mud of the land, scratching at his back and all the bristly sections he couldn't reach. This was part of his rise-and-shine routine, a good roll followed by a good yawn and, preferably, another snack or two. He looked up at the sky. It'd stopped raining, and the sun was on its way down. Darkness would soon descend on the little rabbit sanctuary, offering him cover and shade for his nocturnal loafing.

He heard something... movement, a branch snapping—a potential meal not too far off. "*So verrryy hungry*," he said.

19

Mandy and Sandra were watching TV. Ms. Kenduska had fallen asleep on the couch. Her bifocals careening precariously on the tip of her rabbit nose. Sandra lay on the floor, bent arms propping up her chin, her mettle on display in her posture. Mandy sat near Ms. Kenduska, her eyes glued to the screen. The TV showed a psychedelic man riding a hog (motorcycle); he entered a small town, sundown scenery, a shotgun nestled in a leather case, fitted to his ride. His aviator sunglasses mirrored the world, and a toothpick dangled from his lip. (A preprogrammed commercial—the latest detergent... a new brand name, with all its builders, its surfactants, its bleach—would interrupt the show in T-minus seven minutes.) The viewers were to be taken on a blood-soaked saga, a vengeful odyssey. The motorcycle man had returned to the town that had (five years before) murdered his wife. He was seeking revenge. The sheriff was the supreme baddie, the main culprit, the villainous malefactor; he'd presumably croak last. But before, many more would

die, murdered in cold blood—derelicts and misguided
deputies who'd played their part (or got in his way) would
be hacked and blown apart. The motorcycle man knew no
mercy. He was there to raise hell (or so the voiceover said),
and he walked carelessly and cold, shotgun in hand, down
the town's main street, empty and deserted as the sun
disappeared beyond the mountaintops, and the north-
eastern town sat quiet, solemnly aware that death now
stalked its streets.

20

Tom Wellington was on his way home from the office. Another late night—Tom, the urban planner, drove along the roads, curving his way through the dark forest as his headlights illuminated the bark and branches of the forest's trees.

"Reports of a Jack near Route 36. Authorities caution all rabbits to stay indoors and cease all non-essential travel. Jack is said to have blackish-brown fur and stands a towering..."

Tom was lighting a cigarette, only half listening. He pushed a cassette into the deck and heard Madonna's "Like a Prayer" greet his ears. He kept his eyes on the road. Blackness encased the vehicle. His fuel light popped on, and he cursed his essential laziness. Why hadn't he taken care of his vehicle's menial maintenance at a more suitable hour? He had no answer. Jefferson would be at the nearby service station. He'd be able to fill up, offer a quick howdy to the one-eared rabbit—maybe get himself a microwavable burrito—and make it home none the worse for wear. He took a left and winded around the bend. He could see the illumination poking through the trees—the gas station, the beacon of fuel. The wind blew a heavy gust as he pulled into the service station, and dead leaves flashed across the windshield. He heard the crack of thunder.

While he gassed up, he looked up at the stars. He could only see a few; the rest were hiding from his perspective.

21

Pam and Jim climbed through the opening and entered the tree house; they'd pried loose its door using a thick branch and busted past the lock. Vacation homes and offices were the norm for most of these constructions, scattered around town, usually in heavily wooded and serene sections. The rain was back, and Jim covered Pam with a blanket he'd found... then lightning illuminated the interior—brightness and sharp shadows extended through the cracks in the wood, then the boldness. Boom! Thunder, and it spanned time, it rolled, persisted, stamped itself out—but only after a prolonged moment, a protracted occasion... and Pam crawled to the table and reached up on its ledge and grabbed a candle. She took out her lighter and lit the wick and set it next to her and Jim on the wooden floor.

They could see things nailed to the walls. Notes and pictures and, over in one area, graffiti—written and painted across the space. *I want to write like George Jones sings*, it read. Another said—*Stay hungry. Stay foolish*. And then,

Make good. They sat snuggled up beneath the blanket, candle aglow, storm raging outside.

Pam had gotten hold of Sheriff Huckston; it took three embarrassing attempts (her first two resulted in her being mismanaged by a clumsy receptionist: "Hello…" "Yes?" "I need Sheriff Huckston! Please, it's an emergency…" "One moment, dear…" "*Hello!*" "Sheriff Huckston?" "No, Puck Callwell, how may I help you?" "I *need* Sheriff Huckston! There's a Jack…" "A QUACK?!" "No, a Jack!" "Who's on track?!" "*A fuckin' Jack!*" "Huh!? Speak up, damnit—and don't you cuss at me, lady! Now, please, who's this Quack character?"), and the sheriff had put out the word, and he said he was going down to the Dominguez site with his deputies ("Hold on, Pam. Help's on the way!"). He asked if she was all right, and she said she was fine; she told him to hurry and venture out, go find Jack (priority #1: kill the bastard); Jim had arrived (the dangers abating); they would find shelter, wait out the storm, prioritize a lazy couple of hours outside of harm's grasp as the sheriff and his deputies hunted the beast. Sheriff Huckston said he was sorry to hear about Hymen; he was a good rabbit, and he'd be missed around the warren. Pam was quiet for a few seconds—then she wished him luck and hung up, and then she broke into the tree house with her husband, Jim Kurtz.

Jim held his wife as they lay on the floor, and they watched the light dance against the walls. He kissed the top of her head and was comforted by the smell of her fur. He tightened his embrace, and he felt her sink deeper into his person.

"Thanks for showing up," she said.

He smiled, and then he told her about Mandy and how she got an A on her math test. And Pam said, "The one she was worried about?" and Jim said, "Yeah, that one."

22

"Shit's really setting in, eh?" said Jefferson, and Tom nodded, not feeling the need to engage with the attendant beyond this silent gesture of agreement. He grabbed a bag of salt and vinegar chips as Jefferson hummed a song and refocused his attention on the TV; the rain had picked up; it splattered against the glass windows of the gas station. Tom searched out a suitable beverage, eyeing his options in the back refrigerator; on the TV, Jefferson watched a man with a shotgun enter a saloon and mow down most of those present. He felt he'd seen this movie before, but he couldn't remember for sure... anyway, he was hypnotized by the scene, by the bloodshed, the audacity of it all; a deaf man's dream—he had the volume very low (unlike Mandy and Sandra who had the volume cranked way up... watching wide-eyed even as Ms. Kenduska slept soundly beside them, and the din of the bar and the blasts of gunfire and the moans of the dying reverberated off their living room walls, adding another layer of involvement and sensory overload for the two young rabbits in the thick of their nighttime screening).

It was oddly dim inside the gas station; the lights outside (casting down from the flat-roofed canopy) did most of the legwork and illumination. Tom's car sat rested and refueled at one of the pumps. Jefferson watched as Tom approached the counter, and the one-eared rabbit grinned a toothy smile.

"All set?"

"Yes, sir."

"So the gas... pump two... and these"—he scanned the chips and the pop—"and will there be anything else?"

"That's it, thanks."

Tom pulled out his wallet, scanned his card, and nodded to Jefferson, and Jefferson made a strange bow; his one ear flopped down and bent caustically to the side. And for some reason, it repulsed Tom, and the repulsion spread across his face, even as Jefferson beamed back at him. He grabbed his snacks and left.

23

Bill's eyes were coming around, lids fluttering, consciousness resuming. He was lying flat on his back, and he leaned forward, propped himself up. He could hear someone at the other end of the room—hear water running and metal clinking.

"Hello?"

The sounds continued, and Bill looked around. He saw his leg all sewed up, his wound tied and fastened, secured by thread.

"Hello?" he said louder.

He was on the countertop, cleared of debris; he saw his machines neatly gathered against the wall on the ground. He was still dazed as Doc approached, his casual gait coming towards him.

"It's alright, little buddy. I took care of it. Just rest up. Can I get you anything?"

"No... no, I'm fine. What's going on?"

"You passed out, my friend, and I sewed you back up. You'll be right as rain in no time. Just rest."

Bill reclined himself back on the countertop; he ran his paw across his leg and felt the outline of his raw, inflamed wound, the sutures running across, to and fro. *I really got myself good with that fucking glove*, he thought. He heard Doc at the sink, cleaning something, engaged in his task. He was humming, and then he came back holding a glass, and he said, "Drink this."

Bill put up no fuss and tipped the glass back and swallowed the cloudy mixture.

"Good rabbit," said Doc. "Rest up. I'll keep an eye on things."

But then Bill felt funny, made an involuntary jolt and gesture (as if something had passed right through him), and he spazzed out on the tabletop and felt himself tumble to the floor. He cracked his head, and unconsciousness washed over him once again (his second involuntary brush with darkness). He was out cold, and in his dreams, he saw a doggone monster...

<h1 style="text-align:center">24</h1>

Sheriff Huckston was driving along Highway 6 with Deputy Dean Provost. Their windshield wipers batting like hell to keep the road visible; they turned onto Route 36. The radio was drowned out by the downpour, and Deputy Dean had his shotgun propped between his legs.

"You think we'll spot it, boss?"

"We'll find it. We'll search in teams of two, alright?"

"Sounds good to me, boss."

Deputy Arleen and Deputy Deidra were in the car behind them, speeding along slick roads. They were laughing, rehashing a story from a recent after-work outing in which their receptionist (Julie Meyers) had gotten exceptionally drunk, ole drunken Julie and her boozy outbursts—which included details about Deputy Dean's johnson—and, in a moment of mismanaged enthusiasm (many tequilas deep), she'd tousled Sheriff Huckston's hair, grinning (and gums protruding) all the while. The backlash came in the form of an awkward and hungover morning the following day, eyes bloodshot and head throbbing as the staff each took their turn ribbing the receptionist at her desk; she smiled and tucked her chin and flushed red, offering apologies and excuses ("I just don't know what got into me..."). Deputy Arleen told Deputy Deidra that she'd like to go out with Julie Meyers again. Fill her full of liquor and let her run loose, run wild... Sheriff Huckston flashed his lights and slowed down, and the police cars pulled off the road.

"Ready?" said Deputy Deidra.

Deputy Arleen unholstered her gun. "Why not?"

They had their flashlights out and guns drawn; their slickers ran with water, and Deputy Dean could feel the beginnings of a painful blister developing on the heel of his left foot due to a small hole in his boot and a wet sock. It was difficult for them to communicate with the noise from the storm; Deputy Arleen and Deputy Deidra went left, and Sheriff Huckston and Deputy Dean pushed on to the right. The light mounted to Deputy Dean's shotgun guided them and made strange shadows and effects in the woods and in the rain. Deputy Dean yelled, "Do you see anything?" and Sheriff Huckston shook his head. They pushed on. Deputy Arleen and Deputy Deidra, meanwhile, found Pam's car. They used their flashlights to look inside. Nothing of note, they concluded. Guns drawn, they approached a slanted section, and their boots sank into the mud. Deputy Deidra was the first to see Hymen. She kept her light fixed on him as Deputy Arleen stared at the back of Hymen's head. The rain had soaked his fur, and some of the blood had run off into the earth. He was in six large pieces from what Deputy Arleen could see.

Sheriff Huckston tapped Deputy Dean on the shoulder. He'd found tracks leading off, heavily imprinted in the mud (cloven hoofs); he radioed Deputy Arleen, told her to double back and come meet them.

"How far you think it's gotten off to?" asked Deputy Dean.

"Hopefully not too far, amigo. God, it's really coming down."

Sheriff Huckston raised his head and allowed the rain to smack him in the face. It was coming down in sheets. He watched the approaching deputies move in his direction, beams from their flashlights cutting through the branches, shadows sweeping past.

"Hell of a night for a hunt, eh, boss?"

"Couldn't ask for better."

Deputy Dean pulled at his boot.

"We found the car and Hymen," said Deputy Deidra.

"Okay. We got tracks here. Looks like our Jack's heading out towards Lover's Spit Cove. Deputy Dean and I will take point. Y'all stay back and watch the rear, alright?"

"Yes, sir."

25

Tim Dominguez lay in a hospital bed. Based on what he'd been through and Pam's report, he was kept overnight under the care and watchful eye of doctors and nurses and resident physicians. Sally Hearse was working the night shift, and she'd come by to check on him, holding a tray with microwaved eggs and green Jell-O.

"How you doing, little man?"

Tim kept his gaze out the window. "Alright."

"I brought you a snack... are you hungry?"

"Thanks," he said, not really listening to the young nurse.

Sally sat down on the edge of the bed. She noticed a stain on her scrubs. Blood? Feces? BBQ sauce? Hard to tell. Bodily secretions and brief (but ravenous) forays, scarfing down food while moving and multitasking, combined to make the origins of a rogue stain damn difficult to pinpoint. She put her hand on his forehead and felt his temperature, more as a gesture of motherly affection than for any real medical purpose. Tim looked out the window at the black forest.

"It's still out there, isn't it?"

"Well, it might be, but I know the sheriff and everyone else is out there looking for it. This'll all be like some horrible dream someday, Tim. You just get some rest and let the others worry about it. You are safe and sound now, okay?"

He nodded.

"Eat," said Nurse Hearse. "I'll come back and check on you soon. If you need anything, just hit that button there, hon, okay?"

"Okay."

"And try and get some rest."

26

Bill's dreams were wild. Infused with Doc's cloudy concoction (and a possible concussion... or was it something else?), he was sitting in an apartment—he knew he was high up, pushing past clouds into thin, crisp air (floor 267, he supposed). It was night, and the entirety of the window was black—but he felt the height, glimpsed it in his body's intuitive know-how, the alien feeling one knows of being well above the bounds of where he or she should ever (naturally) be. The couches were old, brown floral designs streaked with red, emitting a musty, lived-in odor. A coffee table with a small bonsai tree was located in front of him. He sat with his paws together seemingly waiting for something to occur. He turned his head and looked around calmly... slowly. Art filled the space, bright gashes of violent color adorned the walls; most of the paintings were small, but one in particular caught his eye (a skull, almost cartoon-like, with its jaw jutting out and paint dripping around the canvas's multicolored tapestry, measuring (as Bill guessed) some sixty inches across). He looked at it for a long time; he felt it move, and even in the context of the dream, this seemed odd.

And then he noticed it, far off in the depth of the black window, a red spot coming towards him. Its presence growing within the pane, and Bill observed it from the couch. Eyes and a volatile mouth floating, it soon took up the entirety of the frame. A spherical monster bumped against the glass. Bill watched. The creature did it again, this time harder, forcefully. Bill could hear the glass fissure, give way as cracks appeared and extended across the surface. *One more go should do it*, thought Bill. And it did, and Bill stood up, and with glazed eyes, the dumb mug of the monster floated towards him, stared at him, measured that which stood before it. Bill did the same. In a lofty chamber high above all else, a rabbit and a monster locked eyes, held captive in the thick of the other's (softening, stupid, and possibly morose) gaze.

27

Doc lifted Bill and propped him back on the countertop. The poor rabbit had smacked his head rather hard, and blood now covered the rear of its cranium, oozing from a small (but rather deep) cut that Doc had just finished bandaging. The cloudy mixture had been nothing but some basic elements (Tylenol, Advil, lemon juice, ginger), crushed and mixed, a soothing remedy (or so Doc supposed), but the fit had proven otherwise, and to add shame to failure, he'd now reinjured his already injured patient, the rabbit... the one who'd freed him and provided shelter and food. *This was not how lasting friendships were consummated*, thought Doc. But maybe that wasn't entirely true, memories of a shared traumatic encounter could perhaps solidify their bond, cuff them to a more permanent and lasting memory of the other, written in scars and wounds, ones that would surely adorn Bill's leg (and perhaps his head) from this point onward. Doc explored the bunker as Bill rested. He wandered the long main chamber and checked the small kitchen (nothing extravagant there), and then he pushed on to a narrow hallway in the back. He crouched as the hallway zigzagged, cut off from the main area's light; he rested one hand against the wall as he explored deeper into the cave and felt the smooth surface of plaster morph into jagged rock, a civilized interior transforming into cragginess, an ancient, weather-beaten hole. He kept on, and the passage narrowed. Doc was on his hands and knees continuing his pitch-black crawl; until suddenly, his journey was halted by a small wooden door. He bumped his head, "Ouf!" He felt around and gripped the handle. It was unlocked. He turned it and entered; right away, he could sense that he'd stumbled into a much larger space. He got up from his knees and dusted himself off in the dark.

"Hello," said Doc.

He heard shuffling, the sound of laughter, a slight giggle—like some childish game was afoot, and he'd just wandered into the thick of it.

"Hello," he repeated.

28

Sheriff Huckston and the deputies didn't find diddly-squat. They sat at Judy's Diner, drinking coffee, warming themselves and drying off in a booth. They had hamburgers and fries and salads and pickled eggs scattered in front of them; the carcasses of chicken wings, piled in a red oval basket, supplied the table's centerpiece. Deputy Arleen licked her fingers.

"We should get back out there soon," said Sheriff Huckston.

"Yes, sir," echoed the rest.

"Maybe... one more coffee, and then we head out."

The deputies nodded in approval.

Deborah Brownshaw came over carrying a fresh pot and topped up the officers' mugs.

"Thank you, ma'am."

"Anytime, Sheriff. Can I get you folks anything else?"

"No thanks. Just the checks, Deb."

"Coming up."

Sheriff Huckston reached in his pocket and fumbled around; scraping the seam for loose change, he gripped a handful of crumpled-up bills and tossed them on the table.

At precisely this moment, Deputy Deidra was whisked off by a thought circulating around her brain—random electrical synapses sounding off. It was about her mother; she'd died the previous year. The memory in question had to do with her bringing another rabbit home. She'd brought Loralie to meet her mother (her girlfriend at the time). Mrs. Deidra had nodded politely during the whole encounter, quietly and elegantly besmirching her daughter's name in her head—her outer conduct though, impeccable. Loralie had expressed her admiration for Deputy Deidra's mother once they'd left (applauded her old-time charm and affectless manner), but a phone call the next day had revealed to Deputy Deidra what she had known all along: her mother was ashamed—saddened that one of her daughters had *chosen* (as she put it) to live this way. Why was she rebelling at such an age, smearing their good name, to get back at her? To get back at her mother that had done nothing but love and care for her? What was the purpose of all this hootenanny? Deputy Deidra had hung up on her, enraged by her mother's rant and the conclusions she'd drawn regarding her daughter's amorous inklings as well as her occupational choice. She ate the last of the fries on her plate and followed the other officers out of the diner. It was still raining, and Deputy Provost's blister had gotten worse.

29

He made cartoons disguised as books. Pam saw this above her head. Another random snippet of text disavowed from what had come before and after it, vivisected and inserted in large font on the roof. She wondered where these words had come from, stolen from other texts, meant to exist as part of a larger whole, or complete and perfect (insofar as was the author's intent) as these short and pithy constructions.

Jim had fallen asleep. The rain had slowed, but Pam could still hear it clattering away outside. She thought of a melody by Vivaldi and allowed it to play out in her head as she watched the candle move and burn. *What a day,* she thought, and then she thought of her daughters at home, confined to the safety of their apartment, and then of Hymen (scattered in the dirt), as she lay in the arms of her husband. The ole scallywag of the office (Hymie), the horny old goat, good-natured and always slightly cantankerous (mostly as a way of undermining his own flirtatious manner); he'd be missed... certainly, but how often had the warren seen this—seen this type of tragedy.

Only yesterday, an entire family had been butchered—then today, Hymen: was this to be their existence? One misfortune following another until the day came when they themselves succumbed to the headline, a short obituary accounting for their untimely demise. What kind of life was this? Was it to be praised or spat upon? A deranged nightmare? An extravagant gift? Did any of them really understand it, anyway? Jim made a short, coarse snort and resumed his rhythmic breathing, in and out. Pam closed her eyes and felt strangely bored by the whole thing.

30

Sally-Joe Buford, too (like Doc), had found the Room—way back in '85, shortly before she and her entire family were eaten by the Jack of their day. She had found it through curiosity, boredom, and happenchance. Bill was not the proprietor of the bunker at the time; in fact, the bunker was initially a storage unit for a large mining company operating east of town. Someone on their board of directors had owned the land and developed the chamber as a means of expansion for the company, a satellite facility only a short distance from the main site (for equipment, repairs, a place to house extra parts at a readily accessible distance). But as the years wore on and the plant expanded, it grew to acquire its own on-site storage facility far superior to that of the little satellite shop; it was therefore disregarded, closed, and eventually sold. In '85, the site still hadn't found a suitable buyer, and it remained locked and vacant, tucked away—a forgotten hole in the earth. Until Sally-Joe and Louise Billworth had found it and made the irresponsible decision to cut the lock (with bolt cutters that Sally-Joe had taken from her older brother, Duke Buford).

Upon entering the bunker, Sally-Joe and Louise observed the decay of the few remaining and corrupted parts; they'd quickly pushed their way to the back and down the afore-mentioned hallway, darkness and claustrophobia seemed of little importance to the youngsters as they pushed and played their way through the ever-tightening corridor—until finally—smack, they'd run right into the small door, and the duo had opened it, climbed inside. And there, for the first time, Sally-Joe had seen (and felt) her first unmistakable brush with the Other—the entity at the end of the hallway: the Room—old and colossal and imperishable... timeless. It stood around her, watching, as she stood within it. She felt that everything had shifted; she was no longer in the land of diners and forests and rabbits and workers—it was as if it had all fallen away, burnt embers and cloaks of ash; and for the first time, she realized where she stood within the anatomy of this place, this darker and more enigmatic design. It had cruelly offered her a new perspective, and once glimpsed, there was no turning back...

31

It was a story about a Room...

<h1 style="text-align:center">32</h1>

"And at its core, it was simply that, a strange hell, a cartoon on fire. And between paragraphs, I drink," said Bill. When Doc had returned to his fallen friend, exiting the Room, he'd found him awake, and he was now exceedingly interested in what Bill had to say, what he had to teach him.

"And more often than not," said Bill, "the answer is 'just 'cause.'"

Doc nodded, not really getting his friend. He figured the bump on the head and perhaps the cloudy mixture of over-the-counter pharmaceuticals had hindered his ability to make sense. But then again, Doc had just exited the Room. He was not the same; his perspective had been altered. What had it told him? What was its secret? Its divine light?

Anybody?

But then Bill got up; he seemed energized, no longer a couch potato with a surgical wound and a bloody head. "This is a playground of madness," he said. "Let's go out, Doc, and hit the town."

Doc cheered on his newfound friend's enthusiasm, and before him, he saw a wave of fluorescent color splash by, disappearing between the walls, circumscribing to a different geometric modality—a span of light peeking through the doorways.

What had the Room told him...?

He grabbed his coat and repositioned his cowboy hat.

Bill tightened his bandage and stretched his leg.

They exited the bunker, and the rain had stopped.

33

Tom was at home, lounging on the couch—TV on; it was the middle of the night. He stood up, stretched his back, and looked out the window at the dark forest below. He saw a white rabbit... Pam! What was she doing out at this hour? And then Jim, hopping along behind her. He sat back on the couch and resumed his television program. He heard the elevator move and guessed the pair were re-entering their abode (one floor up). He heard the creak of the floorboards above him. He turned up the volume.

"Tonight, dear viewer, we have a special treat for you! We bring you a masterwork fresh from the glorious past, one of the mighty gems of cinema. An eclectic trick like no other, filled with..."

Tom looked over at his refrigerator, and, from the distance, he made out a photo of him and Jean, a former lover and friend, stuck against its front. The photo was a year old. *Gone were the glory days*, thought Tom. At work, a fellow employee had come forth and accused him of inappropriate sexual conduct (a recent development that had darkened his mood considerably). Tom the rabbit, while out after work sipping cocktails and having a laugh, had—in the heat of drunken lust and horny shamelessness—grabbed a handful of Suzette's bottom while standing at the bar. She'd been wagging her tiny tail (a young and lovely new hire), and Tom (older, crueler, and considerably more desperate), who, up until that point, had been a charming conversationalist and a pseudo-confidant to the young rabbit, had moved in and done it, taken an illegal moral leap, intoxicated by the beauty, the lust, the drink, (the decor?). And the senior urban planner had squeezed her small and shapely ass, and the sinking feeling of crumbling serenity (*alarms sounding off!*) manifested itself as an abrupt silence—a halt in the two rabbits' friendly and flirtatious exchange. She didn't immediately move away but had tensed and her face froze— and the obvious stutter in her line of dialogue ("I think Joe's really got something to say, wait until next fall when he (*hand grabs ass*) r-r-really...") along with the long, uninterrupted pause (*beat*), should have been enough for Tom to immediately amend his error, remove his paw, and apologize (perhaps even lie and offer a frivolous excuse: "*Sorry, Suze, I slipped... this stupid back of mine...*"), or become all bashful and red, but no... not drunken Tom, doubling down on his efforts, he'd winked at her. Had he not been so drunk, he thought, he'd have never added that callous final touch, that stupid, degrading Hail Mary, probably never would've grabbed her ass in the first place, but here he was, dealing with the issue weeks later, still clinging on (as best he could) to a job he'd all but wished away only a month before, taken for granted—but without it, what was he? His identity in the warren was just that: Tom the Urban Planner. Now, what was it? Tom the Perv, Tom the Monster, Tom the Disgrace. He wasn't sure what the future held. But it certainly looked grim.

34

Doc followed behind Bill. He could spot more blood on the bandage wrapped around his head. It was absorbing it at a rapid rate, and when Doc asked if he was all right, Bill said, "Fine, fine." And he kept forward, a strange madness in his eye; Doc followed closely behind, watching for random branches lit only by the glow of the moon. Bill stopped suddenly; he turned and hurled around and grabbed Doc.

"And do you know how I do it? How I create them? My *stories*?"

Doc shook his head.

"I have a ghostwriter," he said. "A goddamn ghostwriter... she lives between my ears. True story, Doc. How crazy is that shit!?"

Doc said, "Crazy," and made an approving face.

Bill nodded, smiling slovenly. "Yup, *fucking* crazy, man."

Bill laughed and Doc followed his friend's footsteps, chuckling along as they made their way through the dark woods. A frog hopped in front of their path, and Bill snatched it up, quick as a cat, and started licking it. He offered it to Doc, showcasing it for the man in the cowboy hat; Doc extended his tongue—slimy, smooth, and salty—and then Bill tossed it aside, careless of where it landed, its purpose complete. It bounced and rolled along in the dirt and in the detritus, and then Doc saw it straighten itself out. *Ribbit!*

Doc could taste the porous amphibian as they continued their walk near the swamp. Doc spit and rubbed his tongue against the roof of his mouth; he could feel it going numb. A branch cracked, and Bill said, "C'mon, man."

Doc saw the neon glow of the sign peek through the trees, a red outline highlighting their arrival.

"Ready?"

Doc nodded, and they walked up to the club; a red-carpeted walkway led them to the wooden door. The whole building had a repurposed feel to it, as if it'd once been a fast-food restaurant, then converted, its innards gutted, a new coat of paint and a flashy new logo added—and voila!

Bill pushed the door and wandered in. His confident swagger balanced with his bloody head and slight limp should have made him stand out amongst the club's patrons, but when Doc got inside of the Belting Bird, he saw that the remaining clientele was of a similar caste, which Bill could easily maneuver within without any fear of being reprobated. At this hour (which Doc guessed to be around 2 or 3 a.m.), the few remaining drunks all bore some visible foibles or were too far past the markers of decency and sobriety to care who sauntered in, bloody and bandaged or not.

They got a booth near the back and immediately went about ordering an arsenal of drinks: four or five apiece. A group of young, attractive rabbits sauntered in. Scantily clad (one donning a short dress, the cleft of her lower buttocks poking out—and a torn left strap, a red tassel dangling limp down her back), Bill's eyes fell upon the seven new drunken recruits—females of a voracious type. Bill waved, and one looked over and giggled.

A moment later, Doc laughed; he was beginning to feel the hallucinogenic effects of the frog. He took another sip of his negroni, and Bill waved over the slutty rabbits. They giggled again, and Bill raised an untouched drink, offering it as a form of bribe or a token of friendship. Doc looked over and another wave of color rolled through the bar, this one blocking out the entire radius of what had just been visible. When he came back around—reality re-entering the scene—the rabbit in the red dress was sitting between them.

"You know," said Bill, "you're really somethin'. Look at you and your pals out having a good time. Enjoying the fruits of youth. Gallivanting about... not a care in the world."

Bill moved over towards her, his bandaged head covered in blood. He took a deep breath, ready to embark upon yet another mediocre run of groveling and sycophantic praise. Then she interrupted him, switched gears and told him about her old love. The rabbit who'd gotten away. Her former lover who'd taken up with another youthful beauty—and before the universe could be restored, ties refastened, wrongs righted, he'd impregnated the bitch. Crystal was her name. Crystal the homewrecker. And before either Bill or Doc could comment, the young rabbit burst into tears (sobbing between words: bitch... Crystal... Ted...). Bill downed the rest of his drink and waved over the overweight waitress.

"Another round, madam."

And that was the last thing Doc remembered; he fell asleep, and suddenly, he was back in the Room. And a great big voice cut through the darkness. Told him to look, to see, to become what he must become... To look for the rooster—tie himself to that entity, embrace his inner cock. And a sharp pang cut through his head, and his eyes burst open. And in a darkened field—one hundred yards from the Belting Bird—he stood alone. (Had he sleepwalked this far? All the way out here?) He took an uneven step forward and slipped, and that which lay beneath his foot shot out and into the air; it caught itself on a bare branch of a towering aspen, hanging limp. Doc approached. A rubber mask... A chicken mask! He took off his cowboy hat and placed it over his head. His eyes peering through the slits and he heard the Room speak to him again. "Good boy, now tie it up and tie it off." And he felt an impulse shoot his neck forward, direct his musculoskeletal system left. There was a barbed fence, and he saw a long, spiraled section—coiled and cut—lying near the post. Doc walked up to it, propelled by a sense of all-knowing instinct... by the ancient whispering of the Room. He took a couple of yards of the snipped barbed wire and began wrapping it snug around his head, against the latex, against the bone, against his brain; he felt the barbs cut deep into his flesh, graft itself, mixing and mutating in swirls of gore. This was no desultory plan. Somehow, the Room had a purpose here, a meaning behind this horrific disfigurement. Doc continued (wincing with pain) until he and the mask and the sharp metal wire were one.

Doc wandered back toward the Belting Bird; a bloodied latex piece of poultry, he pushed open the entrance doors, smiling between the rips and the wire and the blood (a portion of his lip detached and fell to the barroom floor); he stumbled in and saw Bill making out with the red dress rabbit from before; he was grabbing at her boobs, each of them shamelessly going at it. Doc sat down next to them, dripping blood (slivers of his skull shining through), and the young lady rabbit momentarily detached herself from her lusty embrace and glimpsed (dirty, disfigured) Doc, and it wasn't long before she let out a piercing scream, and she ran, skedaddled, leaving bandaged Bill—the drunken, lonely mess—and he looked up, slow and wavering, and the nonplussed rabbit met Doc's gaze.

"Where you been, cowboy?"

35

Jim woke up first; he looked over at his wife, drooling and breathing evenly out and in. He kissed her and rolled out of bed. He would need to wake the kids up, prepare breakfast, get on with his day. He put the coffee on and entered his daughters' room. "Up and at 'er, ladies," he said. Mandy groaned, and Sandra darted up, ready to meet the day in her usual headstrong manner. Jim entered the kitchen; the sun burst in through their apartment windows. He poured coffee and set about making the girls' breakfast.

Pam could feel the aches and pains resurface in her body, reminders of yesterday's events. She would have to go into work, speak with Jean, talk to Sheriff Huckston, see what was happening with Jack (was it dead, rampaging, hiding, gone?). She was not excited. Jim entered their bedroom holding coffee.

"Rise and shine, sweetheart."

He set the coffee down next to her. She smiled.

"Are the girls up?"

"Yeah, they're having breakfast."

"Good, I can drop them off today."

"No, don't worry. I'll take them down to the bus. The car's still out at the site, I think."

"Oh, God, you're right. I'll pick it up later today."

Jim kissed her head.

"Thanks for the coffee, sweetheart."

36

Deep in the woods, Doc woke up; he heard a slurping sound, and he felt pain extend across his face, and then he opened his eyes, and he came around slowly. He was on the forest floor, and it took him a while to understand the meaning of the image in front of him. His head ached, and he could feel the tears running across his skin as he tried to maneuver his jaw. The wire cut into his fresh wounds and part of the latex mask obscured his vision. But even that... the pain and surprise and regret of defacing his own face were secondary to that which held his gaze. A sunny day and a distended jaw (horribly large) of some beast, slowly ingesting Bill fifteen feet away. Bill was completely out; his preeminent battle within the clutches of death was nothing but a drunk's final unconscious drift towards whatever was next—the afterlife or the thing that came after. Comically mundane, an anticlimactic end... more common than most would ever concede, and Jack arched its back, and like a snake defying logic, reason, and anatomical possibility, it had him in its clutches; Bill entered its stretched mouth (halfway engulfed within its jowls). Jack's eyes shot sideways towards Doc as it held its head steady and continued to pull Bill deeper into its throat. Bill's eyes were closed; he was now neck deep inside the beast, and then the beast performed a quick final slurp and sucked him in, vacuumed him up, and Doc tried to stand up, help his friend. But Jack rushed off, darting through the trees just as Doc was able to get to his feet. *What the fuck*? he thought. He became nauseous and wavered in his step. He fell before a small basin of water. He saw himself in its reflection. The goddamn chicken mask staring back at him, blood dried all through his front and down his face. A crown of metallic thorns wrapped around and cut across, a parody of cartoon violence. What had he done? What was going on? And what the *fuck* had just eaten Bill? He steadied himself and wandered off into the forest. He needed medical attention and an array of drugs, anything to offset the pain and nausea and confusion befuddling his mind. He staggered under the morning sun and stumbled off deeper into the woods. He yelped as he went along; he was an animal in the depths of a horrible hangover and a disturbing scenario.

37

Jefferson was emptying last night's coffee. He'd slept in the back on his bunk for a few hours in the break room. Now, he was back, manning the counter for the morning crowd. The smiling gas station attendant, ready to greet each customer in his ceremonious way. His one ear flopped to the side, and he poured himself a fresh cup. He waved to Liam who passed along outside, taking his traditional morning hop to work. It was a beautiful day, and it only annoyed Jefferson all the more.

Jefferson found little to like in the community of rabbits surrounding his little gas station. He smiled and watched his neighbors enter and exit; it was rapidity and routine. And in their eyes, he saw their verdict; the way they saw him, and thus the manner (if he were to be accepted or amalgamated) that he should see himself. The illusion of status presented in the gaze of each customer—each look cast securing him near the bottom rung (and if not the last peg of the ladder, his place resolved resolutely near the last of the line). Perhaps the winos and drunks were beneath him, but even them, in the midst of their chaos and comedy, offered possibility and chance, something that could easily overtake him. He was steady, dependable, and therefore easily forgettable. Replaceable, likable, and ignorable—the perfect attendant, the greatest phantom, an absolute fucking nobody. *Fuck 'em*, thought Jefferson, and then he heard the gas station's door open, and he turned to face another routine interaction.

But... before he could properly assimilate the visuals, in a midriff spanning momentary delirium, Jefferson remembered his broken dream hailing from a few nights before. He'd been waiting eagerly for a reply (a letter it seemed), to propel him from obscurity, towards success and maybe even happiness. A tiny postman had sauntered up to him, handed him the news carefully sealed in a white envelope. He tore it open, read it quickly, heart racing... then falling. The news: dreadful, degrading, banishing all hope in a few declarative sentences, and then he saw his father walking towards him, smiling, jovial and kind, filled with love; he waved to his son and neared him, ready to greet him, embrace him—ignorant of his disappointment... of his failure. And Jefferson, caught in a wave of despair, felt the toils of heartbreak morph into the adrenaline of anger. He pushed his father whose face betrayed both confusion and hurt—wanting only to understand his son... to help him. His father fell to the ground, and Jefferson got on top of him. He landed an assault of punches against his father's face, blooding him, and his father watched him from the ground; never once trying to retaliate, he simply looked up.

And that thought—milliseconds in the making—gave rise to Doc, standing inside the gas station. A bloodied chicken man in a strange suit.

"*Hello*?" said Jefferson.

"Aaaaaaaaahhhhhhhh!!!!" said Doc.

38

Julie Meyers had had enough; she was packing up her desk, leaving town. A fucking Jack running wild... that had to be enough. She put the last of her knickknacks in a cardboard box (photos, pens, assorted office accouterments) and walked to Sheriff Huckston's office, ready to deliver her letter of resignation. The smell of a fresh pot of coffee wafted through the station. She nodded to Deputy Dean as she walked past him. He stopped momentarily, thinking hard of something to say ("Hmm... take care and good luck, eh, Julie."). She kept walking and gave a small wave without comment.

Sheriff Huckston was seated behind his desk.

"So, this is it then?"

"Yes, but I wanted to say thank you..." She put the letter neatly on his desk, balancing the cardboard box in her other arm.

"No need. It's been a pleasure, Julie. You know, we're going to get this Jack. Another day or two. I've talked to Richard over at—"

"No, Sheriff, it's fine. I just feel like I need a change, you know. Now's the time."

"Whatever you think, but know you're always welcome back."

For some reason, Julie felt a lump in her throat, the sentimentality surging due to the proximity of her exit. Sheriff Huckston's kindness being a bittersweet reminder, unpacking old doorways and memories—a final goodbye aimed at validating a sense of closure, erasing the boredom and tedium and the minor accumulation of workplace spats, and thus allowing her to leave the station on a supposed high note (a fiction... an ending comparable to the denouement of a forgettable (if not goodhearted) holiday drama or a family-friendly and saccharine matinee, tying up loose ends by mawkish and forced means). Sheriff Huckston stood up and extended his hand.

"Best of luck, Julie."

Julie drove south. She was going to visit her sister and her husband a couple of warrens over. She curved the familiar roads and thought about time, about how the goal of life— regardless of paths chosen—always seemed to find itself within the clutches of mass murder. Each member groomed in the fanciful art of killing, devouring and slicing off one millisecond after another, and the accumulation of corpses (memories and trinkets) was the basis for how each life was to be celebrated, viewed, despised; and the style in which an individual could elucidate their deathblows (procreate seedlings and inspire mimics, display their corpses, transcend and hijack the supposed definition of "what a life could be") was, according to Julie, the very crux of societal success. How gruesome and efficient one could deploy their guillotine rendered their rank, often usurping the message of what it was to be alive here and now in this place, epitomizing it, describing it, redefining it...

Tick *fucking* tock.

She was stopped at a red light. She looked left and watched the trees. She wondered about Jack and the corpses... the carnage. She looked at the time, and then the light turned green, and she drove on; continuing her journey, she cut away the moments, each one disappearing, vanishing in her wake. *How would she kill the rest of her time?* And she figured she'd let the corpses decide, past moments dictating coming attractions, the building blocks of the future (Father Time and his magical *horloge*), or something like that.

39

Jack is hunched over taking a shit. His curved spinal column aids the digestive passage. Bits of the Dominguezes, Hymen, Gina, Bill, a physician from St. James Hospital, and an assortment of others fall from Jack's rear end. Hair undigested from Hymen's mustache clings to a piece of Jack's fecal matter, and the sludge of biological waste is a friendly reminder to all that in the end we all go back to the earth, *pulvis es et in pulverem reverteris*, all the same shit returning to the same place. In through one end, out another. One has to see the humor in that. One has to find the madness and grotesqueness interesting, if not attractive. Even if it means succumbing to a less moral point of view, one more aligned with the truth of the world, with all its ridiculousness and horror. Its inherent silliness, its goofiness, its loudness and capriciousness, and perhaps even its maliciousness. To know that comedy is the lame cousin once removed from abject misery, cosmic abrasiveness, endless monotony, and phantom dread. Although in the realm of nearness, serenity and stillness (the calming balms) are never quite beyond the possibility of the next few moments (however infinitesimal the probability), the hope of a speck of transcendence... a perfect unforeseen hiatus, but such things are rare, cultivated through luck and rogue figments of earnest feeling seldom exchanged in the modern world (at least not in plain sight, anyway), and usually requiring the hand of some divine deity to intercept and ignite. Chance or Fate being the final gods surviving amongst most of the Western world. The remaining torchbearers.

Bits of air escape Jack's butthole as he walks, trudging on the reddening, crisp leaves piled along the forest floor. "*So verrrryy hungry,*" he yawns, his cadence slow. He looks for a good shady section for his nap near the base of some tree.

40

Jefferson didn't know what to do. The figure had suddenly appeared, entering through the doorway, making strange demands for drugs between moans and ineffable articulations of pain. "Aaaaaaaarrrggghhh," it said. Jefferson reached for the phone, but something about the flailing arms of the thing, with its grotesque face wrapped in wire, made him put down the receiver. His one ear flopped to the side, and Jefferson motioned to the creature to sit. He had a joint in his pocket, and he grabbed the creature's arm (so enfeebled with affliction) and escorted him through the store and around back. He placed the joint in Doc's mouth, who was able with great effort to open his trembling lips, and Jefferson lit the joint for the fowl-masked figure. Doc inhaled, smoke exited his mask and out his torn nasal cavity. He sat down and leaned against the gas station. Jefferson went back inside and fished out two expired Percodan from his bag and a bottle of water; he came back carrying the pills and placed them in Doc's hand. With a small swig, Doc washed the pills down and carried on with the joint. He placed a hand on Jefferson's shoulder, panting lightly. A show of affection between the disfigured Doc and the one-eared rabbit.

"Aaaaaaaarrrgghh," said Doc, "th-th-thanks."

41

Mandy looked around. The classroom, in all its grandeur, was momentarily devoid of an authority figure. Stuart threw his eraser at Bob, and Bob cried out as the combo of fine pumice and synthetic rubber hit the back of his head. Molly drew an assortment of flowers, etching them around the edges of her journal; her mouth cocked to the side, glasses refracting the light, imagination and inexperience toiling away, unbridled concentration passing the time. Mrs. Banderas had excused herself, called to the office, left the younglings to their own devices. The reprieve, a catalyst for the rambunctious and rogue, a moment to gayly commit as much mischief and mayhem as the instant would allow; then the teacher re-enters her domain, a lapse in the overseer's duty, uncertain of what had occurred—presumably indifferent to it. The news delivered to her in her absence... the real hook. *It was rare to be left alone*, thought Mandy. A breach in typical school protocol; the mood in the class remained light and ridiculous, but when Mrs. Banderas returned, her face solemn, her request spoken quietly but with urgency. All resumed their pose, their attentive stillness.

"Children," she said, "please listen."

Kids sat up straight, eyes and ears forward; even the most callous perked up, the break in sustained authority a reset in their comportment. Mrs. Banderas looked worried. Problems vetted from other areas of the school, now being regurgitated (and presumably censored, reconfigured) for the minds of her young class.

"Children, has anyone seen Kristen today?"

The children all shook their heads. A small rabbit near the back dressed in a unicorn sweater raised her hand.

"Yes, Tilly?"

"She never showed up for the bus today, Mrs. Banderas."

Worry and paranoia (a schizophrenic expansion) manifested in Mrs. Banderas' eyes—although her face remained rigid, stuck in a kind of stupefied daze.

"Thank you, Tilly."

42

Kristen had gone out the night before to visit a friend only a small hop from her home located in a curling hillside subdivision called Mission Heights; she'd left her house sometime around 1 a.m. Her parents were deadbeats—hucksters with an aggressive cocktail schedule that started each morning around 9 a.m. They paid her and her siblings little to no attention. They usually passed out sometime around 11 p.m. *That's how the cookie crumbles*, she thought. She was a smart kid... precocious in many ways. She was the sum of her superficialities. An aspiring writer, wanting only to be next in line, usurping that insufferable Bill. She didn't like the direction he'd taken them in; she preferred a slower trot to his lackadaisical pace and zigzagging style. He was forcing the warren down a hole it wasn't fit to go through. A punishing rhythm, anachronistic and without modern warrant, divergent to the point of subterfuge. These were her thoughts anyway... were they accurate, true? Who the hell knows? But she had anger and fight and acid coursing through her veins, and perhaps that was enough. For in the end, it was fuel. And one often had to utilize the inventory on hand—talents, terrors, desires, any and all hot-blooded emotions, whatever could be yielded, provided, produced. It was as simple as that. Remix the code by any means necessary: kill, kiss, love, canoodle—bend it, reshape it, break it… whatever. *A writer's credo*, thought Kristen. She was deep in the forest now; she'd taken a shortcut through the heart of the woods. At home, her mother turned to her father, both waking from alcoholic dreams.

"Where's Kristen?"

"Fuck if I know."

And sometimes she thought she'd write a book just so she could burn the motherfucker, for warmth and light.

43

Bill was gone, dead, digested. Jack had put an end to him, consumed him as fuel. He'd gone from drunk, high, stoned, and unbalanced to no longer part of this world. He didn't wake up; his consciousness had simply vanished. A trick. Here one minute, gone the next. But if he had woken up, where would he be? And in some ways, he did wake up, but what awoke was hard to characterize as Bill. A mist, a vapor, that's what it looked like. It floated through a temple. A vibrant pinkish-purple fog, drifting, glittering through the space, past incidents and memories and ancient columns and rats; the vapor pushed on, weaving and floating among the invisible currents of the cavern. It contained little of Bill's personality and no note of his appearance. It was *essence absolue* though, twenty-one grams of purified soul. Bill personified. His dust and particles moved along through the air, through the Room. He drifted through a door, down a corridor, between walls; he made it into a small factory: there was a rabbit on a table and a cowpoke holding a glass. The rabbit drank, and Bill the Mist drifted through the rabbit; he felt its innards, its goo, its psyche, and then he was out of the workshop. There was a crash, then trees, then fresh heavenly air. He moved, evaporated, slowly mixed his molecules with those of the outside world and re-entered the game by once again being digested by it. One part per million mixed here and there with the forest and the rabbits and the monsters.

Home sweet home.

44

Kristen felt it first. An eerie feeling as the fur on her neck stood on end. As she wandered down the well-trodden path, past tree limbs and gnarled branches, she could feel something's gaze, measuring her motions and movements. She was only two minutes from Drew's house, but something told her that she wouldn't make it in time. A detour was needed. She could hear it, panting, a ruffling behind an elm. Dead leaves crunched; emissions rose up above the shadow of some creature.

"Hello?"

She sensed its position, but then a sound behind her spun her around and all orientation was lost.

"Who's there?"

She imagined the scent of its breath, rotten teeth and gingivitis—eyes punctuating the darkness; and again, she heard the crunch of the creature stomping and stepping. She should run; she knew it. She eyed north, hopped fast, darted in the direction of Drew's house. Ducking past branches, they scraped and lashed at her. She heard it behind her, in pursuit. She pushed forward—faster, harder. She navigated below a fallen poplar tree. But then her leg was stuck, caught between a crevice in the tree and a rock. She could see the silhouette approach. It unglued itself from the darkness, stood tall above her. She winced, fearful of the approaching being. "*So verrrryy hungry*," she heard. Its cloven hooves stepped on the poplar and pressed her foot further into the crevice. She no longer had to imagine the foulness of the creature's breath. She was pinned and awaiting the teeth that would soon tear into her, rip her apart, snap her neck with devious and intuitive joy. But—as luck would have it—a shot rang out. A loud crack that momentarily pulled the beast's attention away from her. Distracted by the sound, Jack looked out, and another crack resounded. Jack growled at the darkness, and Kristen tucked further into herself, hastily trying to pull at her leg and set herself free. Another crack—this time louder, closer. Jack bore down on the tree, and Kristen screamed. Another crack, Kristen shut her eyes, and pain climbed along her nerves; the terror numbed her, froze her. But then she felt the tree lift. She opened her eyes, and Jack was gone.

She waited in awe. *What had just happened*? Was she all right? Dead? She heard footsteps coming her way, methodical things. A turtle entered her field of vision; he knelt beside her, a shotgun draped over his shoulder; he fumbled with her foot.

"Almost got it, dear."

She felt pressure as he pulled and pushed her foot, and then she was free. She pulled herself out from under the tree. The turtle sat down next to her.

"You alright, miss?"

"Yeah." She was still a little disoriented, in a mild state of shock. "Is it gone?"

"Yeah, it's gone." The turtle checked the chamber of his shotgun. "That sombitch's sure a lucky sombitch. It's pulled me all over this damn county. Been here, there... Hell, I don't even know where I'm at anymore."

"You're chasing that thing?"

The turtle laughed. "Yeah, well, everyone needs a hobby. It ate a surly neighbor of mine. I took a shot at it and missed; then, well, I kept after it... and have been ever since. Lucky for you too, or that thing might've got a nip of the ol' rabbit tonight." He laughed again. "Let's get you home, little one."

"What's your name, mister?"

"Pete, you can call me Pete."

Pete helped Kristen up, and he told her he'd accompany her home. He asked her what she was doing out so late, traveling alone. "Ain't no time for a rabbit to be out, miss—young or old, you hear?"

Kristen nodded, acknowledging the turtle's slight reprimand, and then he changed his tune, asked her about the warren. Was there someplace decent to stay? To eat at? He had a hankering for some good late-night chow. He asked if she was hungry, and she nodded. He said he'd buy her a piece of chocolate cake (a post-traumatic snack), and the two set off towards Patty's Diner.

45

Kristen took him down a shortcut through the swamp. The path weaved along a narrow strip, oscillating past the trunks of submerged trees. Pete eyed the frogs and kept on the lookout for any alligators. He pulled out his pipe and went to work puffing away.

"This here is a nice swamp," said Pete.

Kristen agreed. "I like coming down here," she said. "Not many rabbits venture around these parts. It's a nice way of getting around the warren without having to deal with too many undesirables."

Pete nodded. He wondered what she meant by that, but instead of asking and firing the conversation off towards another new tangent, he went quiet; his attention was directed elsewhere, towards the far bank. Between the trees, two figures appeared, talking loudly, moving in stops and starts between the tupelos. It seemed unlikely that the pair had seen them. Pete touched Kristen's shoulder and motioned for her to quiet down. He pulled his shotgun off his shoulder and bit down on his pipe. He watched them through the reticle. A bandaged rabbit and a swaying man? The tall one was wearing a cowboy hat, and the rabbit seemed to be licking a frog.

"I think that's Bill."

"The tall one?"

"No, the rabbit," said Kristen.

Pete squinted into his scope. They were heading in a similar direction and their paths would likely converge at some point down the road. Pete asked if they were dangerous, and Kristen said unlikely. Pete lowered his gun and kept an eye on the pair as they walked. Kristen started up again, asking the turtle about the particulars of killing Jack, and then she asked him where Jacks come from, and how Jacks become the way they do and end up in warrens, particularly this one. Pete smiled. "No one really knows where they come from. Legend tells of demons, possessed personnel that were physically once very different. Infected and broken down, they reconfigure themselves in their new fur, accompanied by an insatiable appetite. Little rabbits are said to make great Jacks, turtles too, for that matter." He laughed again, but Kristen didn't know what was funny. They continued along the swamp path, and Pete noticed that Bill and the tall fella were gone. They re-entered the forest and crossed the road; no cars, just a flickering streetlight down the way. The lights were on in Patty's Diner, and Pete pushed the door and held it for Kristen, and they took a booth by a window. The waitress brought Pete a coffee as he perused the menu; her heels clicked across the checkered floor as she walked away. Kristen eyed the posters and photographs of famous animals hung against the wood paneling. A rabbit on a stool whistled an unmelodious tune before allowing it to die mid-chorus;

Pete looked out the window.

46

"So, you'll kill the Jack and then what?"

"Head home, I suppose."

"Hmm..."

They ate and sat for a long while, and Pete noticed Kristen's eyes heavy with sleep, her fork laid down near the small remaining clump of cake.

"You ready to get out of here?"

Kristen nodded, and Pete directed her to the door. He paid and nodded to the waitress, and the two animals re-entered the night.

"Which way's home?" asked Pete.

Kristen pointed south, and Pete said, "After you, little one."

They took a path through the forest, tight and winding, and then it opened above a sloping clearing with trees scattered here and there. The moon colored the land in a pale blue tint. Kristen got on her stomach and rolled down a part of the hill. Pete smiled—and in the distance, he caught sight of two figures: Bill and the tall stranger.

"Is that them again?" said Pete, more to himself than Kristen. He pulled off his shotgun from his shoulder and looked through the scope. Sure as shit, Bill the bandaged rabbit... but the other one seemed different, had lost its cap—perhaps even its face (its identity? Its destiny?). "Hey, Kristen?"

"Yeah?"

"Stick close to me, okay?"

"Alright."

Pete watched the two figures; they stumbled here and there among the glade. They seemed drunk, lopsided; Pete wondered where Jack was. He watched them wander through the clearing, clearly having trouble with the slanted ground. Kristen stood beside Pete, and they walked down the hill at a slow pace.

By the time they arrived near Bill and Doc, both characters had fallen over drunk. Bill was laughing and talking to himself, rolling near a forgotten basin, genuinely out of his mind on whatever the two had ingested that night. The other, when Pete flipped him over, was sound asleep. Kristen recoiled at the sight of poor Doc—wrapped in barbwire with his chicken mask. "What the heck's going on here?" said Pete. Pieces of Doc's face leaked, and the wind shook a torn flap from his mask. *What makes a fella do something like that?* thought Pete. *This is sure one strange fuckin' forest.*

Kristen nudged up against Pete, and he told her it'd be all right. He searched Doc's pockets and found his wallet. He opened it. His license said his name was Dirk Harttright. The picture was of a handsome man, quite the stark contrast to the gruesome sight before them. Pete pocketed a twenty from Doc's wallet before returning it to his pocket.

"Let's get out of here. If these two sorry sons o' bitches want to lounge about in the grass and get eaten, so be it. But we're gettin' out of here. C'mon, little one."

He lightly prodded her on and followed the young rabbit out of the clearing. Something howled behind them, and the rabbit and the turtle pressed on.

47

But they didn't make it far before trouble reared its ugly head again. Pete had his gun in hand as they made their way through the woods. He heard branches cracking. The sense of being stalked weighed heavily on each of them. It was almost assumed that they'd have another run-in with Jack before the night was up. It was the way of fate—a lulling intermission, then back to the action. A turtle and a rabbit versus a bona fide killer. It provided good fodder for the story. Kristen gasped, and Pete aimed his shotgun, and Jack advanced. Gunshots rang out. Growls, hisses, roars. But in the end, savageness and baseness won out. Jack came out wounded by a ricochet, and Kristen and Pete ended up in pieces, dismembered, eaten, ripped apart. The last thought Pete ever had was, *"There are no happy endings here."*

48

Jack burped. This was turning into quite a feeding frenzy; his shoulder was bleeding from the shotgun pellets, and his abdomen was distended from all the good eats he'd been ingesting lately, particularly in this last 48-hour stretch. Neither situation slowed him down much, though. It seemed like easy pickings here. Jack would round a corner or dip into a nook or cross a bank, and just waiting there was another being ready to be devoured. Jack moved through the forest and into a clearing. Two bodies rested on the ground. Jack was full, but he knew he shouldn't pass up such easily accessible prey. "*So verrrryy hungry,*" said Jack, even though he wasn't. He opened his mouth near the bandaged rabbit and stretched his jaw, engulfing the thing, inhaling it in one slow mouthful, taking his time as the rabbit was pulled into his esophagus and down into his belly. Jack saw the other one move, wavering slowly on the terrain. He continued to eat, keeping one eye fixed on the waking creature. The man tried to rise but shuddered, and Jack slurped up the final bits of the rabbit. Too full or careless to contend with the disfigured man, Jack moved on and set out on its way, back into the depths of the forest. The sun had risen.

49

Doc was with Jefferson now. The Percodan along with the joint had helped, calmed him, allowed him a moment to put the physical pain behind him and concentrate on the emotional burden of what he'd done and mull over the last few hours. He thought of the barbwire as a tornado that had snuck up unannounced and singled him out, lined him up on its path, and dug in, tearing him apart. He knew his life would immediately change; this was a sign, perhaps from God, or the devil (or the entity in the Room); whichever way he looked at it, some divine force had cracked his life in two, and he was now entering its second phase. Jefferson handed him another bottle of water, and Doc said thanks. Jefferson returned to his store and left Doc out back sitting on a wooden box. Doc sat staring at the sky, and he wondered what he should do; the pain was easing; Bill was dead, and he was a monster—well, perhaps not a monster, but he had the makings of one, the outer shell, which, when he thought about it, made up a good percentage of what people took to be monstrous. Obviously, if he were to fully immerse himself into his new form, he should bear the disposition of the beast, homicidal whims and a reckless proclivity for violence, complete the picture. But Doc was not a monster in the traditional sense; he knew this. He didn't have the bearing for that type of senseless destruction. He would be a meek monster, shying away from the world, rejected on the basis of his looks. Perhaps over time and with enough rejection, he'd assume a more violent demeanor, regress to a more palatable and stereotypical freak, align himself with the initial perceptions and first impressions that he was sure to inspire cloaked in his new mask. Time would tell. He stood up and started walking back through the forest. His shoulders slouched, and he vaguely recollected the way back to Bill's bunker. He followed his feet.

50

Sheriff Huckston and Deputy Dean were scouring the woods, a daytime search. For all their tenacity and resilience, they had been unable to come across Jack. All they kept seeing was the carnage in its wake. A pileup of violence and death, but it was strategic, it seemed, at least to Deputy Dean. They were walking and enjoying the peacefulness of the forest, when all of a sudden they'd find signs of a struggle, a piece of a dead rabbit or animal, then back to the calm, typical, day-to-day sights of the forest. A peregrine perched on the top of a pine tree. It eyed the two officers below before it flew off again.

"You think we're going in the right direction?"

"No clue," said the sheriff. "We'll keep this up for now. Kristen's folks said she probably came this way."

The officers continued their search. Sheriff Huckston figured that Kristen was probably dead, but he never liked to admit defeat until all the evidence was gathered and laid out before him. His instincts were of secondary concern to the sheriff; proper procedure and facts, logic and reason, these were the ways to do police work. All the mumbo jumbo about the policeman's intuition was nonsense from what he could tell. Follow the clues, the footprints, the violence, then dispatch the cause—arrest it, kill it, cook it and eat it, present it to the town, prepare a feast. Whatever was called for. Whatever needed to be done.

51

Doc swung open the door to Bill's bunker and descended the steps. He acted instinctually, without prior thought, simply doing what his body commanded, separate from his mind. It was like his head was stuck in a bowl of water, floating independently above this mechanical thing that moved and made decisions of its own accord. It was staggering to Doc to note that he really wasn't in control of his limbs; things were happening without him. He wasn't even a passenger, just a vantage point on top of a moving hill, at least that's how he thought about it; glimpsed through the slits of a torn Halloween mask, he watched as his body grabbed items from Bill's workbench, piling them in its arms. Building up towards something, but what? And although he (from his point of view) wasn't making any decisions, he certainly felt the weight of them, as his arms were soon filled with items, bulky things. He walked through the bunker. There was only one small lamp left on, and for some reason, it made the place seem romantic. He made his way down the corridor, walking this way and that, working his way through the narrow passage. He got to the small door and nudged it open. The Room was as black as ever—but then he noticed, to his left, a table and a chair, lit overhead by some unknown source. His feet made their way towards it. Doc set down Bill's typewriter, a stack of paper, a mug, and an ashtray. He pulled the chair out and sat down and cracked his knuckles. As he played the keys, he saw the type hammers get to work, and every now and then, a rogue bit of mechanical debris would stab at his hands and fingers. Small notes of blood made their way into the machinery, greasing the gears, keeping everything fluid and afloat. His bleeding mitts kept at work, and his eyes blinked dumbly as the words appeared across the page.

52

Doc's Tale:

It is cold out. Minus thirty-five degrees Celsius, far too cold for any creature to be out in. Such cold is the antithesis of life, of movement; how could one dare face such an entity? All he could do was turn on the TV, plug in the goddamn thing, flick on the screen, power the portal, sit by the heater, submit to the signal. Dick wasn't sure what was on; he'd browse in an upward direction and allow his fancy the chance to pull some image from the wreckage and allow his mind the opportunity to follow its sequence for a brief while. Tune out his seclusion (his solitary existence) by basking in another's story. A promenade down another's lane. It was a cartoon. A clown milling about in a picturesque forestscape. It was two-dimensional, a cel-animated epic. The clown was drawn with a bulbous nose, a pointy hat, and darkened lips. From what Dick could tell (jumping into the show, ignorant of all motives and happenstance that had come before), the clown seemed nervous or scared, but not so scared that it wasn't continuing on, pushing forward, exploring the terrain. The muted landscape was doused in heavy fog, a layer of some murky shade that drifted strangely from left to right and then all but disappeared without any consideration for atmospheric verisimilitude or the angles of the drawings underneath. Dick supposed budgetary considerations as well as time constraints may have accounted for this (although artistic choice or general laziness may have also played a role). The clown kept on through the shrubs and past the trees. He came upon an opening, and he witnessed a network of rising buildings, hexagonal in shape, push upward from the soil. Dark marbled constructions ten or eleven stories high, he approached the base of one and stood on a platform. He saw a panel with strange symbols decorating its transparent façade; he pressed the screen, and the platform began to rise. The clown rose on the side of the building, watching as his open-air ascension propelled him high above the treetops. He drifted past the layer of fog and then out into the blue sky. The glare of the sun was nearly intolerable as it ricocheted off the black cathedrals scattered throughout the land. The clown continued to rise, and then suddenly, the platform halted, and he stepped onto the roof. He walked to the door near the roof's edge and opened it; he took the staircase down. Dick had yet to hear the clown make so much as a whimper; he was not a vocal character, but his movements seemed to betray certain characteristics; he had a sly gait about him.

The clown entered a room where a man dressed in a brown three-piece suit sat behind a large desk. He was bald and wore a great big mustache. He said, "Sit," and motioned with his hand towards the chair in front of him. The clown took his place, and the man continued on. "It is nice to see you again, very nice indeed. We got a job for you. He's a chippy one, but we'll pay you top dollar. Scout's honor." The clown nodded, and the mustache man said, "Wonderful, right this way then." Both men stood up, and the mustache man held the door for the clown. He winked at his secretary as they passed; she let out an aggressive giggle and sheltered her eyes. They took the elevator, and the mustache man pressed the number 8. The door opened, and they exited and walked the corridor. A few people busied themselves, carrying folders and papers and burdens and corporate memos in their heads and hands. The clown and the mustache man pressed on, and then the mustache man said, "Here," and he opened a door to his left, and the clown walked inside.

A clown, a killer, and a dwarf all stand within the Room, and the mustache man says, "Welcome, one and all!"

53

Meanwhile... on the other side of town, Jefferson called Sheriff Huckston. Once he'd realized that the defaced chap behind his gas station was gone, he figured, based on all the known weirdness arising of late, that he should let the sheriff know. He wasn't sure how much good it'd do, but he felt compelled to call him for some reason. It felt important in the domino effect to come.

"Howdy, Sheriff."

"What's the trouble, Jefferson?"

Jefferson explained about the man he'd found and the cut-up manner in which he'd found him. Jefferson was keen to note that the disfigured fellow seemed nice enough, apart from the obvious derangement emanating from his fucked-up face and his limited use of speech. But one couldn't rely solely on outward appearances or conversational imperfections these days to justify a man's guilt or fault; look at Jefferson, for goodness' sake, he was downright ugly and deformed with a penchant for platitudes and nonsensical sayings—and, from the town's point of view, there wasn't a rabbit more beat up and unappealing to the eye and ignorable to the ear than the one-eared gas jockey. So, Jefferson had his qualms about casting stones at the man in the chicken mask solely on the grounds previously discussed. They were brothers of the misshapen lot. But, for some reason, he'd called up the sheriff anyway.

Sheriff Huckston asked if the man was still around, and Jefferson told him that he'd wandered off an hour or two before; he wasn't sure in which direction either. Jefferson could hear the sheriff sigh; he thanked Jefferson in a half-hearted way and told him that he'd keep an eye out for any freakish fellas, although his plate was quite full at the moment with Kristen and Jack and all that murdering and mayhem and missing rabbit business going on in the warren. Jefferson thanked the sheriff and hung up. He then rearranged the bags of chips before some youngsters entered. He rang up their purchases, and then they drifted out. He stared up at the muted TV and watched a dwarf swing an axe at some low-level fiend. He was feeling very listless today.

54

Tom sat at his desk at work. Due to the recent rampages, his inappropriate conduct (grabbing Suzette's ass) seemed to have diminished in importance. Its stench still lingered at the office though, caught in whiffs as coworkers grouped together in small cliques and eyed him in the hallways, speaking in low tongues and judgmental quips. He figured he deserved it. The gossip and grouping and exiling were typical of the pack; it seemed appropriate that he should be hated, ostracized—barring Suzette and all that, he still felt that his lot was to settle on the other side of the aisle, separate from the regular sort bulwarking the morals of the workplace. He couldn't put his finger on why, though. He called it a spiritual separation—but that was just a place-holder until some better term or colloquialism arrived. Did he like being an urban planner in the warren? Yes, for the most part, he did. But he never felt particularly involved in a social sense with the rabbits around him—be they coworkers, acquaintances, nemeses, bosses, or friends. *Did he still have friends*? He needed to think that one over. What was the qualification for friendship nowadays? The gap seemed to have widened over the last while. Typical Tom nights involved a take-out meal, cigarettes, cheap wine, and hours of frivolous television—and, all in all, he was fine with that (repetition didn't necessarily discount happiness); and whenever he had to break the chain of habit and rendezvous with some old so-and-so, he couldn't help but feel bothered and annoyed, if not downright angered, at having to tear himself away from the comfort of his apartment, put on an amicable face and a pair of pants, and greet some fool whose interests and troubles held less importance than the fictionalized sufferings on his much-maligned TV shows. Booze was the only way to get through these meetings and hangouts. Balance the scales of drunkenness against the dullness and reproachfulness of the speaker. Hangovers be damned! It was often the only recourse left.

Suzette walks by and smiles at him; Tom is so taken aback that he stops dead in the hallway and spills half his coffee all over his blue sweater. He hears a song about a pink moon coming to eat you; it's coming from the nearby office. He mutters, "Fuck," and walks into the women's bathroom to clean himself off.

55

Pam was sitting in Jean's office. She was telling her what had happened, the whole Hymen episode—and Jean was filling her in on Sheriff Huckston's failed attempt to capture or kill Jack. News of Kristen's disappearance had also made its way into their conversation. They drank coffee, and although the chitchat centered around pressing issues and downright dire events, the caffeine and the coziness made Pam feel good, in tune or entrenched within the conflicts of the warren. In a way, she felt strangely giddy. Yesterday's derring-do had put her face-to-face with the monster, realigning her relationship with the day-to-day. Killers and death often had a reciprocal impact, a way of making those who'd glimpsed them, or touched them, or come extremely goddamn close to them, feel energetic, even euphoric, particularly as they re-entered some casual calm, some comfortable normalcy—although the feeling was ephemeral. Even death couldn't uproot homeostasis for long. Things had a way of balancing out.

"Truth needs to be compounded in order to build up its credibility. Everything is degrees of truth under the right light. You understand?"

Pam did not.

"I'm talking about the need each truth has to lean up against other truths. A network of truths. A giant mechanism leaning up against itself, towering and teetering based on the blocks (truths) inserted—required—to keep the monument afloat.

"I'm talking about the thing-in-itself, you see? The endgame of truth, the giant monopoly of identity hidden at its core. The thing telling it how to stand, breathe, fuck, dance. The core principle shaping it. Truth's DNA."

Pam did not understand, and Jean said, "Oh, forget about it. This whole mess has me rethinking everything, every available fucking morsel of me seems to be uprooted. I can't handle anything right now. This Jack isn't just a physical torment, it's an ontological one."

Jean grabbed her mug and tipped its contents back. Pam sometimes wondered if it was only alcohol she mixed with her coffee or something more sinister.

"One of the deputies brought your car back. It's parked in the lot. I'd like you to rendezvous with the sheriff and help out with Kristen. Maybe talk to her parents. See if there's anything to find out. Okay?" said Jean.

<h1 style="text-align:center">56</h1>

Jim was lounging at home. The girls were at school. Pam had run off to work. He flipped on the TV. He browsed the channels and tuned in to the news broadcast. He wanted to know how the Jack hunt was coming along. He fixed himself a late lunch and sat back on his recliner. His bologna sandwich flopped carelessly in his right paw; some mayo slopped on his shirt. As far as Jim could tell, no new news had been communicated since the last time he'd tuned in. Jack was still on the run; many rabbits were still missing; the sheriff and deputies were still in pursuit—that about summed up the entirety of the details that the news anchor wished to share with his viewership. Jim supposed more information was out there; in fact, he knew more. He'd seen the damn creature face-to-face, saw its gnarly snout up close, knew its sleeping style (belly down, head perched on claws), knew that it had a salty scent to it, pure black eyes (as Pam recalled), had a slight excess of adipose tissue around its abdominal and groin areas, ate dutifully, and grotesquely played with its food.

While thinking about Jack, his mind drifted... and he thought about love, and he made up a definition, and he said love was intensity over time, and, for some reason, he thought—*Horror is mostly a job for mothers*. He walked over to the fridge and uncapped a cold bottle of pop. He hadn't put on any pants yet; he felt pretty good.

57

Pam got ahold of the sheriff, and he told her to meet him at Judy's Diner over on 6th Street. She found it funny driving in her car that day. The last time she'd driven was with Hymen, and now, the next day, here she was, going to meet the sheriff, in pursuit of the very thing that had eaten her passenger the day before, which they in turn had been pursuing because it had eaten the Dominguezes some hours before that. The car was a mix of things familiar and past, even as it propelled her at speeds topping sixty miles an hour into the future. *A curious little gizmo,* she thought. Inside the car was memory, a string of vignettes, car rides with Mandy and Sandra, date nights with Jim, errands and routine—and outside was everything else, unpredictability, the cloak of chaos, random events unfolding as she pushed by or through, parallel or perpendicular to, a map of atomic collisions weaving all matter, and she slowed down at a traffic light; it dangled from a branch of an overhanging limber pine tree. She lit a cigarette and then tightened her grip on the steering wheel. She thought about calling Jim but decided not to.

She got to the diner, and she saw the sheriff sitting at a booth. She joined him, and he had the look of a ragged beast as if the monsters of the forest were rubbing off on him, turning him sour and foul. But in reality, Sheriff Huckston, like Jim, was thinking about love. He was thinking about Julie, his old receptionist, and he was thinking about those types of mousetraps that glue the little bastards square to the spot; the ones that suffocate them, or induce tiny heart attacks, little rodent collapses, or force them to wait in paralysis, he thought—for the ensuing death blow, the coming end—sometimes waiting for hours, other times, mere seconds. He'd heard that some mice even gnaw off their limbs to escape. He thought they lacked common sense, but certainly not know-how. He was thinking about all this (about mousetraps and love) because he was thinking about how many of his limbs had gone and gotten stuck to past lovers. A hind leg here, an elbow and a humerus chewed off there. Scattered across the land. Portions of himself had been distributed in all corners of the forest. Untethered by flings and one-night stands and long-term relationships and unrequited loves. One was liable to lose every piece of oneself before a suitable trap was found to stick to, to wither and die upon. *Love certainly had its cost*, thought the sheriff.

And the sheriff said, "I just don't see any way that she's still alive out there. I think she's a goner." And Pam hated to admit it, but she thought so too.

58

Deputy Deidra was out with Deputy Dean, and she, like many of the characters at the moment, was whisked off by fanciful tidings, musing on the common theme of love. She had Loralie on the brain again. The diner the night before had unleashed a hellion of emotion, taking form in the memory of a long-lost lover. Here she was, searching for a lost child, lust and heartache and serenity and separation pushing into her from all corners. She walked through a dying wheat field of a nearby farmer. She figured they wouldn't find the kid, and if they did find anything, it wouldn't be anything good. Deputy Dean looked at the furrows on the ground and thought about taking a coffee break. Deputy Deidra was remembering a speech Loralie had once delivered. Espousing a theory about evil, she'd said: "Evil is only malleable once it's been deemed ridiculous. Then it's vulnerable for a short time, like molten glass fresh from the furnace, allowed to be molded and reformed by the glassblower's talent and whim. But, like most things on Earth, this is no easy task. Things are by their nature ridiculous, so ridiculous in fact that for us to see anything as ridiculous—genuinely ridiculous, that narrow balance of playful, pathetic, and absurd—takes great skill on the part of the ridiculer. It's akin to a type of time travel whereby you're traveling through time to retrieve someone's old forgotten eyes, the dead eyes of their youth, and you're allowing those eyes a sojourn, a temporary return; summoned by the ridiculer's words and tone, they stoke the fire, hoping to intensify the flames. They're often unsuccessful, but someone is always trying, and that's what's truly important. So long as someone is aiming their sights on that, on salvation dipped in ridicule, the world will be okay." It was so trifling and stupid an explanation that it'd somehow stuck with her years later. But why was she thinking about it now?

Deputy Dean said, "Coffee time!"

59

Pam went to speak with Kristen's parents at the behest of Sheriff Huckston and Jean. Both thought it'd be a good idea. If not for the case, it was an excuse to get an agent inside. Rumors of abuse and neglect at the Wentworth residence were well known around the warren. Sheriff Huckston had spoken with the Wentworths multiple times already. They were standoffish and rude. And although the sheriff could see that their missing daughter (Kristen Wentworth) weighed heavily upon them, the load seemed to be blunted or aided, as if by some invisible ghost, helping to carry it, the load of sadness and pain and guilt, an invisible family member, a possibly demonic houseguest, even though it was probably doing some good at the moment. *One should never trust these astral aides*, thought the sheriff. He figured some type of alien was nibbling away on them. The sheriff sometimes thought of aliens taking the form of ideas, invading households... these parasitic concepts... secreting drugs, actions, words... but only certain words, and only in certain configurations, and only for certain amounts of time. He figured the Wentworths had one working through them, or on them, living with them—a muscular and deformed thing if only it had a physical form, but no, it remained hidden, a mystery, a slight thickening of the air and a sense of quiet death. That's how it made its presence known; it was a master of discretion and concealment. *It gnaws on you while you sleep,* thought the sheriff. *And one day, you got nothing left; it's eaten all your innards, all your good stuff. All your filling's been sucked out by an idea, or a group of ideas, a shifting idea, words grouped and realigned to take the stuffing clean out of ya.*

Pam knocked at the Wentworths' door, and a young rabbit answered.

"What's your name, darlin'?"

"Samantha."

"Are your parents home, Samantha?"

She pointed behind her to two recliners with lounging rabbits, each an unhealthy offering of fur and despondency. Their eyes had yet to make their way towards Pam; they stared up at the ceiling, somewhat stern in expression. The room was abundant in shades of brown and muted yellow.

"Hello, Mr. and Mrs. Wentworth."

She raised her voice so they could hear.

Mrs. Wentworth looked at her. "Yes?"

"I'd like to speak with you about your daughter."

Mrs. Wentworth didn't move or reply. After five or so awkward seconds, she stood up; her clothes were wrinkled, and the fur on her head was in disarray. "I told the sheriff everything. But you can come in if you like."

She turned and walked down the hall away from Pam. Pam took off her shoes and excused herself as she moved by

Samantha. She gave the little one a forced smile, and Samantha just stared back at her blankly. As she passed Mr. Wentworth, she heard him talking to himself, but then she realized he was actually talking to the cat beside him... but in such a way as if an actual dialogue was playing out. As if the cat was explaining the situation to Mr. Wentworth, giving him valuable intel. He glanced at Pam, suspicious-like, and the cat went back to gnawing on his purple slipper.

60

Tim Dominguez was released that morning from the hospital, and his guardianship was transferred over to his uncle, Curtis Hanshaw. Curtis picked him up in his SUV and took his nephew to his lodging. Unlike many of the rabbits of the warren who'd modernized over the years and set their sights to the skies for their abodes, living in high-rises, condominiums, and tree houses, Curtis preferred a more traditional dwelling. He made his tunnel near the base of a small valley on the east side of the warren and fitted it to his liking, adding rugs and coffee tables and an assortment of found furniture and knickknacks. Curtis was Tim's mother's brother and her only surviving sibling. It was rare to see Curtis around the Dominguez household. He kept to himself, a separate entity, and Tim had always been curious why. His father had once called him a maggot, but he never elaborated on it. Curtis showed Tim around his home; he'd prepared the guestroom for him. Tim was grateful, but all these sudden changes (i.e., once a rabbit among four siblings and two loving parents only 48 hours before, and now the sole survivor living in his uncle's tunnel) left him perplexed and dazed; he shuffled through the burrow without a steady emotional grasp to hold on to.

After the tour, Curtis fixed Tim some eggs and sat with him while he ate. Neither one had much to say (*what does one say to the lost?*). So Uncle Curtis asked Tim what he felt like doing that day, and Tim said, "I'd like to go down to the swamp."

And Curtis said, "Okay."

61

Pam sat across from Mrs. Wentworth at the kitchen table. Their talk hadn't progressed very far. Mrs. Wentworth had trouble concentrating on Pam's questions or totally disregarded them altogether; for some reason, Pam felt that some self-preservation instinct was to blame. As if someone was eavesdropping on them, and if Mrs. Wentworth gave the wrong answer or divulged too much information, some punishment or misfortune would be waiting right around the corner. Her answers were brief and nondescript. Pam watched as the children wandered in and out of the kitchen; she'd counted six so far. All of whom seemed careless and unconcerned by her presence. They were dirty, but they didn't seem unhappy.

The last known location of Kristen Wentworth had been Patty's Diner according to the sheriff's recent report. Apparently, a turtle had accompanied her. It wasn't necessarily odd for turtles to suddenly appear in the warren, although no one at Patty's could identify him by name. When

Pam asked Mrs. Wentworth about it, she said she didn't know any turtles and doubted Kristen did either.

Mrs. Wentworth excused herself and went to the bathroom. Pam sat alone. She browsed their kitchen, judged it while seated at the table, concluded it could've been dirtier. It was well stocked with spirits, and it had a nice size dining table with a napkin holder as its centerpiece. "It wasn't a hellhole per se," was how she put it. Samantha appeared back in the kitchen and fetched herself a glass of water. As Pam watched her, she thought of Sally Buford and the Jack of '85. The stories she'd grown up hearing, the carnage the beast had wreaked throughout the warren. She wondered what it was that had suddenly brought the Jack out. Were there signs written, a proper preceding code that needed to be inputted, prompting Jack to appear, foretelling of his arrival? The Bufords had been attacked on a Tuesday morning, a full-on assault, so many rabbit bits littered the scene that no one could decipher who's who among the remains (a mirroring of the Dominguez incident). It had kick-started the killings. It was the first time in a long time that the warren had faced such a predator, such an entity hellbent on destruction and digestion. It was estimated that over thirty rabbits had succumbed to the Jack during the '85 rampage. They had finally succeeded in killing it; a small posse of hunters had cornered Jack, and bullets rained down, cutting the creature in half. Why was a Jack suddenly back in the warren? There had to be a reason.

Mrs. Wentworth re-entered the kitchen, and Pam excused herself, and she thanked Mrs. Wentworth for her time. As she exited the household, one of the children ran up to her and tugged on her coat; Pam bent down, and little Timothy Wentworth said, "Don't let it eat you, too." The cat eyed her sideways.

62

Jim was going out. It was late afternoon. The girls would arrive home in a few hours. Mandy had band practice, and Sandra had volleyball. Each had a ride home. He had some time to kill, and he donned his old hat and unlocked his rifle from its case. He would go for a walk. A leisurely stroll through the woods armed to the teeth, a wayward wanderer in the form of a formidable opponent. *He felt it this time; he felt it in his blood.* He was going out to meet Jack. Their fates were twisted at this hour. Jim wondered how he knew this. What tingle heightened his senses and professed his assurance in the matter? He shrugged off the question and loaded his gun.

63

Doc was hunched over writing. He couldn't stop. Whatever tentacle had wrapped around him forced his hand upon the page. He was degrees of back, behind the mask and the mind operating of their own accord. He was entirely irrational. That's what he'd succumbed to. An extremist of improbability, citing actions that had no valor or motive beyond some bodily one that forced his vessels to follow its impulses. He wrote in the Room and was dumb to all else.

A snippet of Doc's writing:

"And remember, the devil likes to hide in feelings too," said the dwarf. "He *fucking* loves it there. A despot weaned on salvation and sensationalism, especially in its extreme forms, is the devil's favorite plaything."

The dwarf thought he'd emerged victorious in the matter, but the clown still wasn't buying it.

64

Curtis and Tim arrived at the swamp. Curtis parked his SUV, and the two rabbits walked over to the path weaving along the Spanish moss. The clouds diffused the sun, and a strange overcast glow hung over the land as Tim looked at his uncle. "C'mon," he said. Curtis had the feeling that an illness had settled over the warren. One that had begun as a slight headache, a radiance throbbing through its temples, the onset of the cancer, fevers burning down churches and corporate headquarters alike, leaving behind some cosmic misdemeanor disguised, as what? As reality—some strange place where the abnormal had normalized and confounded the patient, so much so that the delirium was actually encouraged among its internal components (organs). An ecosystem out of whack. *These were strange times*, thought Uncle Curtis.

Tim had wanted to return to the swamp; it was one of the last places he and his family had been right before the Jack attack. They had embarked upon a day of sightseeing. A favorite pastime of Mr. Dominguez. A carefully choreographed routine of routes and pit stops planned according to the degrees of the yellow dwarf star overhead and the unsynchronized bladders of the Dominguezes ("Another stop! For Pete's sake, we *just* pulled over. How come you didn't go then?"). The swamp was first; it had mystique at sunrise. Unlike other times of day when the swamp grew to encompass a sense of decomposition and waste in the minds of the mammals who didn't belong there, these hours welcomed beauty and contrast, sparkles and glimmers; the swamp temporarily dazzled them in her flamboyant dress, fashioned under shifting hues. And the croaking frogs shut the fuck up sometime around 2 or 3 a.m., leaving the morning to the other critters whose songs were soft, lending a subtle movement to the harmony of the scene.

Tim went on ahead, scouring the path and looking for whatever he happened to be looking for. Curtis kept a curious eye on the young rabbit. He wasn't used to being around the little ones and had not questioned Tim's motives for coming out to the swamp. He wondered if he should've been more inquisitive, but that's not who he was. He was one who followed orders easily. Kept his head down and did what was asked. Authority took many forms for Curtis, even an overly pungent thought could ransack him, diminish him for days. He would have to keep his eye on this Tim character for a while, suss him out, feel out his motives. Tim said, "Found it," and raised his arm into the air. Curtis squinted and saw him holding a small toy. He swung his paws through the air in retort—the midges had encircled him; they were driving Uncle Curtis a mite nuts that day.

65

Jim headed west along a well-worn path just outside their tenement building. He had his rifle loaded and in hand. He'd passed Ms. Kenduska on the way out and had greeted her with a smile; she'd replied with a slightly aggressive comment about the weather. The sun had yet to break the barrier of clouds; its inability to defy this hurdle set some folk on edge, as if the sun's incapacity had a more inauspicious application—the failure of the cosmos—light cast being bound and filtered, diffused and tinted, at the whim of a malevolent atmosphere (for even the stars have enemies), a chaotic order enveloping their little celestial prison. It made Ms. Kenduska feel impotent, and she said that word aloud ("impotent") as she walked towards her door. She envisioned flaccid penises, loose rabbit dicks. This cheered her up. She unlocked her door and entered.

Jim's gun hadn't been fired in a while. He figured he should take a shot or two once he entered a little thicker into the bush, testing the mechanisms of the machine. The gun was a precise bomb, an explosion sending projectiles (seven millimeters in diameter) hurtling through space, linear, rotating along its longitudinal axis, a far-reaching wizard's wand casting a single spell: displacement. His phone rang. It was Pam.

"Hi, hon."

"Hey, whatcha doing?"

"Oh, just out for a walk. You?"

"Just finished up at the Wentworths'. Was thinking of ordering in tonight. How's that sound?"

"Good, good. Any news about Jack from the sheriff?"

"No, he's still searching around with the deputies."

"Alright, hon. Well, I guess I'll see you at home then."

"Sounds good."

"Love you."

"Love you, too."

As Jim put the phone back in his pocket, he caught sight of a snake coiled along the edge of the path. He directed his machine at the serpent. Its path of displacement would intersect with the creature, reorganize it, diversify its purpose, expand its potential. And its matter would be recycled, reintegrated, a chemical redistribution, disrupt the flow of the game by removing a participant. The gun symbolized a creative act. The creation of a future where one tiny bullet had reconfigured one small component and thus changed its course. It was an architect of change for better or worse. He fired at the snake. It was separated into two halves. Both ends kept moving as he walked by it. Its mouth was wide open as it twirled in the dirt. Jim wondered what the snake was thinking. What goes through the mind of the recently fractured? What did the serpent think of this divorce? Did the tail think it was now free?

66

Jefferson ate a bowl of noodles behind the counter. The day had progressed around the same lines as any other once Doc had departed. Jefferson found it odd that such a strange encounter could occur and seemingly be swept under the rug by reality, thought of as a minor blip, and reconstituted as part of the new fabric of its structure. Eaten within the narrative of the world, digested and accepted. *Boredom smoothed everything out*, thought Jefferson. He stared out the gas station's large windows; he glanced up at the TV. A deformed man and a bona fide killer on the loose, and still boredom persisted, ennui took hold. He was tired. A customer entered; he perked up—slouched slightly less. Tom went straight to the counter.

"A pack of Kools and a lighter."

Jefferson grabbed the cigarettes and pitched a green lighter onto the counter. Tom's blue sweater had a large brown stain. Jefferson pretended not to notice.

"Anything else?"

Tom smiled; it defused the fact that he hadn't been listening (the two-word question somehow slipping by). A forced smile was how he handled most of the world he refused to pay attention to, either because his mind was preoccupied or because he didn't care to listen to the words. Smiles were weapons too. Grimaces of apathy—gestures empty of feeling; there only to continue the show, progress events in the most civilized way possible with a limited expenditure of emotional currency. Instead of telling someone to shut the fuck up—smile, disengage the neurons. For some, this was a natural response. Hierarchies embedded in the social fabric or cultivated through an individual's unique journey (Who ignored them and who did they ignore? Or perhaps it dates further back, the neglecting habits of their parentage?). Physical traits and reputation privileged certain individuals with airtime, determined the focus and attention they were to receive.

"Anything else?" repeated Jefferson.

Tom smiled, grabbed his smokes, and left without a word.

67

As Tom drove home, stopped at a stoplight, he saw Deputy Arleen and two others scouring the woods. Richard and Willard had driven up from a neighboring warren known as Beaverlodge; Sheriff Huckston had called them the moment he'd confirmed that it was in fact a Jack they were dealing with. Richard was known for his ability to flush out a beast and mount an attack; he'd killed a Jack a few warrens over a couple of years back. Willard was his hand; he didn't say much, but few doubted his expertise. Tom lit his cigarette; he'd left work early, told his supervisor he felt unwell, which wasn't a complete lie. He hadn't thought much about the Jack. His mind orbited other ideas, mostly concerning his own situation in life, which, up until now, had not included a mass-murdering beast. The warren's issues were secondary. Something to be pondered over at work in relation to parks and roads and buildings—decisions he was paid to mull over; apart from that, what went on with the other rabbits didn't interest him much. Days of death and disappearances, civic pride and traditional holidays—the bonds of community, the burden of collective tragedy—weren't topping the charts for ol' Tom. His thoughts had gravitated elsewhere... circling planet Suzette—in some strange way, he felt he'd fallen in love with her. Her celestial body had pulled him in, and he nosedived through her atmosphere, plummeting towards the crash.

68

Deputy Arleen raised a torn bit of bloodied cloth into the air. Using a stick, she waved it around like a patriotic flag. Richard and Willard walked over.

"This here looks like the spot," said Richard.

Willard let out a monosyllabic sound, confirming the deduction.

They had walked a ways into the bush; it was plain to see that this was the spot of some violent encounter. Evidence supported another Jack attack. The three of them spread out and looked around the terrain. Willard made a sharp whistle, and the two others walked over to him. A strip of a sleeve belonging—as far as Deputy Arleen was concerned—to a small female rabbit. They continued to comb the area; not far was the cracked shell of a turtle and a busted shotgun. Richard called up Sheriff Huckston, let him know that they'd found the spot. The sheriff told him he was on his way. Richard lit a cigar and offered one to Deputy Arleen; she politely declined. He puffed away while Willard kept surveying the scene. "It's all part of the plan," he said. He bent down and touched a puddle of viscous liquid lying in a pool. It tightened and loosened between his paws. A raven croaked; it translated as: "That is that."

Sheriff Huckston showed up ten minutes later, and Richard took him around the scene. "Goddamnit," he said as he wiped his brow. "We really need to kill this sombitch, and soon." Richard nodded. "Any thoughts where it might've gone off to?"

Richard looked around. "The best we can do is keep tracking it from here and hope we catch a break, either by finding it ourselves, or some lucky citizen stumbles upon it and has enough time to send out a quick SOS. I hate to say it, but I think we're at the whim of luck on this one. Sooner or later, our Jack will find itself in a tight spot, and then, sure as shit, we'll kill the bastard."

Deputy Arleen overheard the sheriff's and Richard's talk. She felt unnerved by the whole episode. A sense of helplessness crept in around her. She watched Willard who kept wandering the scene. He looked up at her, pointed south, and said, "It went off this way."

69

Tim turned the toy over in his paws as Curtis drove. It was a tiny airplane with a pink propeller. It'd belonged to his sister Dorothy. He remembered when they'd first arrived at the swamp the morning of the attack. It was still dark, their sightseeing tour kicking off under the usual cloak of blackness. Stars and a moon (still as stone), the Dominguez family walked, flashlights in hand, taking the weaving wooden path. Corine and Dilbert led, followed by Mr. and Mrs. Dominguez, Martha walked behind them—deep in thought—followed by Tim and Dorothy in the rear, chatting and playing and horsing about; she kept her brother busy, showing him her new toy and engaging him with nonsensical questions; she loved her brother a great deal. Dorothy stuck her paws into her pockets and stopped dead along the path. Tim was the first to notice.

"What's wrong?"

"I dropped it."

"What?"

"I dropped my plane."

Tim had his flashlight pointed at her. The rest of the family stopped, turned to see what was going on.

"I'll go back with you."

"No," said Mr. Dominguez. "We'll pick it up on the way back. It'll be light then."

Dorothy was reluctant, but Tim prodded her on. He gave her a wink and pulled out a pack of gum. He handed her a piece.

"Don't worry. I'll find it for you."

70

Doc heard something. Sounds were strange in the Room. Things didn't necessarily add up. It was as if inside sounds (imagined scenarios, internal sonic amplifications) transformed into mechanical radiant energy—pressure waves moving through the air. But then there were sounds he hadn't imagined; things breaking in, disruptors of concentration. Pausing the narrative process, halting it, pulling Doc out (a momentary reprieve before pushing him back in). The silence of the Room had initially tricked him. It invited noise, required it. He heard his own blood moving and coursing through his veins and then a young girl's distant voice; these words coming from the Room were typically unintelligible, or Doc had lost the ability to decipher them even as he smashed away at the typewriter before him, using this very medium of language (verbs, nouns, prepositions) to pronounce his tale to the world, playing it with the frenzy of a possessed marionette. The light overhead—guiding Doc's writerly journey—had dimmed considerably; he wrote with little understanding of where he was, what he was doing, or who he'd become. Writing here seemed to cleanse him of his personality. It swallowed him up. Allowed him to overstep his limitations as a man. He was the medium composing the medium, and yet with every word, he felt himself fade, drifting further and further than he'd ever wanted to go. The man in the chicken mask kept on, and he wrote, "The clown was not made for this. And yet, through no fault of his own, this is where he'd ended up. Somehow fate had rewritten his wiring, plucked his feathers and recalibrated his machine. The mask reintegrated, permanently engineered itself as the face."

71

Jim's meander through the woods had taken him a mile or so from his home. He scratched between his ears and tilted the gun, resting it against his shoulder. He hadn't passed anyone since Ms. Kenduska at the onset of his journey. He watched the squirrels running, hopping, and skipping along among the many trees. He thought of his daughters, Sandra and Mandy, and his wife. He would soon kill the Jack—or Jack would kill him, or he'd continue his stroll, find nothing, and loop around another mile or so down the trail and head back home, no better or worse than before. He peered through the forest, saw nothing, and kept on. He kicked at a stone along his path, and he watched it skid off down a slope to his left— and there, a black smudge caught his eye, about a hundred yards away near a brook. Jim bent low, crept along the foliage, careful to ease his way over the odds and ends of the woods, making as little noise as a rabbit could. He moved within fifty yards and tucked behind a tree. He heard it talk. "*So verrrryy hungry,*" it said.

72

Deputy Deidra and Deputy Dean were driving when they heard the shot. Sheriff Huckston had radioed them only five minutes before about Kristen Wentworth; it'd put each of them in dour moods. Even though this only confirmed what Deputy Deidra had felt in her heart all along, the tragedy lurking around the bend, although before it seemed to have disguised itself, associated with worries and concerns related elsewhere. Yet it was the confirmation of Kristen's fate that had brought on a profound melancholy that she hadn't expected, solidifying the narrative in such a way as to render life in the warren in a new light—a gloomy brightness. She still had Loralie on the brain though; the memories of her former lover hadn't been completely shaken but had mixed with the tragedy of poor Kristen and come out newly tinted, a fresh wound again. Tragedy and pain had a knack for repeatedly digging in the same spot, carving fresh wounds in old scars. Loss compounded, then grew numb—only to reinsert itself anew, reborn in the blood of another. She felt for the Wentworths, for Kristen, for the warren, for her mother, Loralie, herself, and even Deputy Dean—she felt winded when she heard the bang of the gun. At first confused, she'd thought it'd somehow come from somewhere inside, expanding outward from her core.

"Who the hell's shooting?" said Deputy Dean.

He slowed the patrol car; they heard another shot.

"This way," and he sped off down the road.

Deputy Deidra unholstered her gun.

<h1 style="text-align:center">73</h1>

Pam entered their apartment; no one was there. She knew the girls were still at school, and Jim must still be out, gallivanting this way or that. She sat on the couch and thought of where her daughters might be at that precise moment, which lesson was being spelled out for their rabbit ears. Numerical sequences, linguistic tirades, mercurial codes—symbols articulated and bound together by a collective thread, each with their place within the curriculum associated with the preplanned development of the youthful rabbits, sculpting them under the banner of acceptable norms. She heard a knock at the door. She got up slowly and opened it. It was Tom.

"Hi, Tom. What can I do for you?"

"Sorry to bother you, Pam. Do you have a minute?"

Tom'd heard the Kurtzes' door above his apartment open. He wasn't sure if it was Jim or Pam who was up there. He'd hoped for Pam, but Jim offered his own brand of folksy conversation, too. He was all wrapped up in strange feelings, romantic intrusions, a guilty conscience, and he wanted someone like Jim or Pam; someone prosaic, of a caliber similar to himself to chat with, if only for five minutes, to shoot the shit in such a way as to cast a spell of normalcy over what had suddenly felt like a bad dream descending over his existence. He would ask questions about Jack, the kids, her day, ask if he could borrow a spatula or a rolling pin—it didn't really matter; he just needed time... time defined under the parameters of ordinary chitchat, a surefire remedy, or so he hoped, for the disequilibrium he felt all of a sudden. Sitting alone in his apartment had only aggravated this feeling, this seasickness. He covered his mouth and burped and already felt a bit better.

"Yes, of course. Come on in."

Tom entered, and Pam pointed him to the couch.

"Would you like a cup of coffee?"

"Only if you're having one."

"I'll put on a pot." Pam walked to the kitchen and turned on the faucet. "How's work?"

"Good, good. How's the Jack hunt coming?"

"It's coming. The sheriff's confident it'll all be over soon."

"And then the feast?"

"So it seems."

The coffee machine beeped three times, and Pam re-entered the living room and sat next to Tom.

"You're getting chubby, Tom."

She pointed to his midsection. He laughed.

"And how are the girls?"

"They're lovely."

Tom thought back to the days when they'd grown up together. In many ways, she was the most prized rabbit of her time. She was certainly beautiful, but it seemed to extend beyond that. She was brave too, and self-sacrificing, even-tempered, quick-witted; her enviable traits were numerous. He had often thought about what it would've been like to marry her. To extend his bloodline with Pam's and watch the amalgamation form into new beings with the best and worst traits from each of them battling it out for supremacy. Over the last while, he had tried to dissolve these feelings and thoughts. All attempts had been futile.

74

The first shot missed. *Fuck*! thought Jim. He aimed again; it was coming right at him; he wedged himself between a cluster of tightly packed trees, hoping the barricade would hold. He fired again. He heard it wail; its fluid spilled out, dark liquid pouring out from below its ribs. *Goddamnit*, thought Jim. *Go down, you sombitch*. The shot had slowed it, but not enough to inspire much confidence in Jim or his shooting theatrics. Jack was damn near fifteen feet away; Jim knew it'd have trouble with the grouping of trees—*just too goddamn big, it was*. Jim tucked himself in the far corner near the trunk of a cedar tree; a sharp bank rose up behind him. *If this is to be my last stand*, he thought, *so be it*. He fired again and missed.

At this point, Jim dropped his gun. Jack was closing in, thrashing through the trees and upending branches and bark; it was torso deep between the cluster, clawing and swiping at Jim, who knew there was no exit. A shot rang out from elsewhere. And then another shot. Jack sprang backwards, let out a shriek of pain. It retreated before Jim could understand what was happening. He grabbed his rifle and clambered out from his tight spot.

He walked out and saw the Jack move towards a small hill near the roadside; he heard more shots. Two separate entities were firing. It took Jim a minute to come to his senses. He aimed his rifle at the hind side of the creature and fired—he hit the left side of its buttocks. It wailed but kept forward. It moved like a crab, circling, unsure which direction it should charge. He fired again; Jack turned and darted for him. Jim ran back towards the cluster he'd just extricated himself from. He fell into it and scraped his cheek against a broken tree limb. He scrambled, still clutching the gun. He fired without aiming, without coordinating, the butt of the rifle jammed against the ground. The shot sent the rifle twirling through the air, somersaulting upwards as the bullet entered the uppermost region of Jack's skull. Its body dropped, and its pink brains seeped out of its cream-colored skull. It continued to gurgle a few words. Jim got up from the dirt and pulled himself out from the trees. Jack followed him with its one functioning eye. Pools of black and silvery liquid spewed forth. Jim picked up his gun and watched Jack breathe chaotically for a few moments. When he felt ready, he fired another round into Jack's head. He saw Deputy Deidra and Deputy Dean walking towards him.

"Nice shooting, Tex," said Deputy Dean.

75

Tom and Pam were enjoying their second cup of coffee when they heard the radio.

"*Reports are coming in that Jack is now dead. It seems a shoot-out has just occurred over near Berrybrook Farm. Deputies were quick to respond to reports of gunfire. One citizen along with two deputies are responsible for bringing an abrupt end to the vicious saga of Jack and his reign of terror. We spoke with Sheriff Huckston who had this to share: 'We would like to express our gratitude to the citizens of the warren for their bravery and trust during these uncertain times and would like to extend our heartfelt sympathies to the families and friends touched by the tragedies over the last few days. Our thoughts and prayers are with you.' A feast will be organized to celebrate the end of Jack. All ages are welcome, and the event will be held at Pickmore Park tomorrow evening starting at 3 p.m. with activities organized for the little ones... Now a word from our sponsor: Good times, bad times. Anytime and all the* *time, everyone is happy when Ringo's around. Come join us at Ringo's Toy Emporium, where we have all the hottest offers... like $14.99 for the new Toads of Infinity action figure. Hurry as supplies are limited... Good times, bad times. Anytime and all the time..."*

Jim opened the door; he had blood running down his cheek and the black blood of Jack on his hands. He held the rifle by its barrel in his left paw. Neither Pam nor Tom said anything, surprised by his appearance.

"Howdy, Tom. Say, is that coffee I smell?"

"Are you okay?"

"Fit as a fuckin' fiddle."

Jim tongued around the roof of his mouth and felt his dogtooth wiggle. He sat in the recliner opposite the pair, his rifle across his lap. No one spoke for a moment. The radio played an elegiac piano riff. Jim felt good; he knew his daughters would be arriving home soon safe and sound. Pam got up and went to the kitchen to grab another cup of coffee. Tom said: "Did you kill it?" But Jim didn't answer. His mind was racing in circles, recalibrating the narrative, restructuring his story. He smiled at Tom and wiggled his tooth.

76

Once Horace heard the news, he told his wife he was going to lie down. If he could even get three hours of shut-eye, it would make a big difference. He knew the call would be coming soon. It would be an all-nighter. He had his wife lay out his knives and cleavers. He would sharpen them upon waking with his whetstone. But only after he took the required measures of rest. He snuggled under his duvet and grunted. The end of Jack and the beginning of his role within the festivities. He heard the phone ring and his wife answer. The predictable sequence of events unfolding, resumed order had blotted out the short-lived chaos of the monster. In some ways, he felt disappointed—it wasn't that he wished for death and destruction in the warren, but now, in hindsight, when he'd seen the full story, perhaps he'd expected more... and then it all resumed, the colors were put back inside the lines, the monster defeated, another blip in the game. He tried to calm his mind, concentrate on his breaths. He wondered what Jack's insides might look like. Would its heart be near its intestines, kidneys where lungs typically were? He'd never butchered a Jack before. The Cookbook mentioned that Jacks were rarely identical. Organs were moved and transported, rewired according to God knows what. Its outer shell remained typically unchanged, but inner configurations were numerous. An anecdotal incident even mentioned a Jack whose liver was somehow tied to its sigmoid colon. He tried to keep anatomy out of his mind but ended up dreaming of a giant excavated nervous system, an extension of spindly wisps attached to a swelling brain and two round, googly eyes. It was laid out for miles along a desert road, and he drove along next to it, and a crow kept pace overheard. His alarm beeped; the three hours were up. He reported to his knives and got to work.

77

The sheriff poured himself a coffee and topped up Willard and Richard's cups.

"Well, that about brings an end to this Jack business."

"Sorry we couldn't've been more helpful," said Richard.

Willard looked out the window of the sheriff's office. He saw a few deputies wander past. Dusk was settling in.

"Nonsense, I appreciate you boys making the trek. It means a lot. I hope y'all are staying for the feast tomorrow?"

"Well, I suppose we could."

Willard grunted; the sheriff couldn't deduce what the sound signified, but Richard remained pleasant, firm in his choice.

"I'll set you boys up at Murweather Lodge for the night, if that's to your liking?"

"Sounds wonderful," said Richard.

Deputy Deidra knocked at the door. "Yes, Sheriff."

"Deputy... yes. I wanted to thank you for your work and bravery. How are you feeling?"

"I'm good... good. Happy we could put an end to it."

"Is Deputy Dean with you?"

"He's just out front; I'll go and grab him, Sheriff."

"Thank you."

The trio of rabbits sat in silence. Richard smiled and remained pleasant amid the setting. Sheriff Huckston racked his brain for something to say, and Willard mouthed, "It's all part of the plan," under his breath.

Deputy Dean arrived.

"Deputy, thanks for coming by. I wanted to extend my congratulations to you and Deputy Deidra. Thank you for your wonderful police work."

Deputy Dean blushed and acted all bashful. Willard did not acknowledge Deputy Dean; instead, he watched out the window, and far in the west, he intuited the coming storm.

"Just doing my job, Sheriff."

"Well done, Deputy," said Richard.

Deputy Dean excused himself, and Richard stood up; Willard followed suit. They shook hands with the sheriff and exited the station.

"What do you think of all this, Willard?"

"Something's rotten in Denmark."

78

Tim couldn't sleep. His monster was dead, and it'd had nothing to do with him. It wasn't that he even wanted to avenge his family per se, but somehow he thought his story with Jack would amount to more. It seemed suspect to watch how something could come and go and leave your life in ruin and then up and expect you to make sense of whatever was left, the so-called "untarnished and untouched," even though everything was different, recontextualized. He played with Dorothy's toy; he spun the propeller, and he listened to the thunder outside.

<h1 style="text-align:center">79</h1>

Doc kept hammering the keys. From time to time, the Room made rumbles, like a stomach pleading for more. He had something to do with feeding it; he knew that. Yet he wasn't sure which type of chow it subsisted on—all he knew was that his role was to smack away at the keys. Clack, clack, clack. Sometimes, his eyes would move upward, away from the page, and he'd notice the Room changing, morphing its dimensions. He glimpsed a set of double doors across from where he'd entered—but later, in a brief moment of recollection or clarity, he looked towards them again and saw nothing but blackness. The voices he heard in there confused him too, and Doc could no longer make out whether they came from the Room or from himself. It felt like the Room rotated, a dubious carousel—a circular ride with a motorized core and oblique ornamentation. He kept writing, fueled by an unknown purpose. The dwarf clown in his story (the heir to power and fame and fortune and bad luck and trickery... a coming together of two separate personalities) had wandered into a nearby town, persuading and hypnotizing the populace with its serpent tongue. Conjuring prizes and gifts for the fools of the town as they were quick to embrace their new pint-sized hero.

An excerpt from a few pages back:

The dwarf looked at the clown sitting around the campfire, the glow dancing across the makeup of his shell. Once the clown was asleep, the dwarf would make his move. He'd use the large rock he was sitting on to smash his skull. And then he would steal it; he would unmask the clown, use a scalpel around the jawline, remove the flesh, take up residence, and thus mobilize the face...

80

Sandra sat on her father's lap; it was already 11 p.m. The news of Jim's victory over the Jack had spread fast, and once the girls had arrived home from school, they jumped into his arms, proud of their father and curious about the tale he had to tell. They wanted a firsthand account of the event, the paternal take on the defeat of Jack. Both girls were held by the story, no less for the fact that Jim broadened it somewhat, paving over facts with more interesting tidbits and fanciful constructions, tightening the pace of the narrative. Pam had heard it from Jim when he'd first come in bloodied, fresh from the kill—both she and Tom were all ears. The phone started ringing off the hook thirty minutes later; thus, she witnessed her husband's courageous battle with Jack pass along the gossip channels of the warren and morph into myth and fabrication as Jim expanded and erased and censored his own story (switching out bits here and there based on the reactions he received... trying to express in his words the best possible articulation of his tale while still being within the realm of verifiable facts). He allowed the story to choose its own desired shape; over the coming days, it would settle in. The proper sentences would coordinate and crystallize, and from that day until the day he died, he'd be able to regurgitate the defeat of Jack at will and with very little effort. It would have henceforth found its style, its structure, its most fitting form. And all he'd have to do was stick to the script.

81

Horace was reading the Cookbook; Jack was spread out across four tables that had to be pushed together on account of its size. As he read, he patted the surgical saw against his side, already eager to get to work, to cut into this creature, to make liver stew, dissect its flank, smoke its ribs, roast its rump, and remove its thymus gland (saving that bit for himself and the missus). When he'd first entered the workspace and seen the size of Jack, his heart had jumped. *Cooking this bastard would be no easy business*, he thought. The Cookbook wasn't particularly helpful on how to start; diagrams were fashioned based on what was discovered, namely focusing on the locale of three particular organs (heart, kidneys, lungs) as a way of situating the butcher within the parameters of Jack. But first, he needed to skin the creature; it'd already been hung and bled out in the woods, hoisted up and dangled. He grabbed a knife and cut into its pelt, keeping the blade pointed away from the carcass; he started around the hock joint of its left leg. His right hand (knife hand) was his clean hand, and his left hand worked at tearing away the hide; he cut at the skin and the fat and worked his way towards the core of the Jack.

82

When Pam finally settled the girls down and got them in bed, she was hoping Jim would be running out of steam. He'd been talking at a furious pace, large circular sweat marks hung around each of his armpits. She loved him, was proud of him, but he was also starting to annoy her. She felt bad that his victory had spurred on such feelings. Perhaps she could tire him out by making love. He sat on the edge of the bed, huffing and puffing, the mental excitement manifesting as physical drain. She caressed his back, danced her paw around his thigh, maneuvered across the groin, and grabbed his pecker. He shut up immediately. He turned, and they kissed, and they made love, but her plan was a failure. Once they'd finished, he ramped back up again. Talked voraciously, spoke of an uncle from a far-off warren who'd have fallen right out of his chair if he knew what his nephew had done.

"Uncle Patrick would not believe that little Jim could track and kill a Jack. Jeez Louise, to see the look on that asshole's face..."

Pam lay down, exhausted by her husband's inability to remain silent. She flicked off the lamp near her side of the bed. He jabbered on in the darkness.

83

The black blood of Jack was proving difficult to work with. Horace had never worked with anything like it, and the Cookbook made no mention of any special properties, but each time he was in there, cutting around, he felt the blood pull and push, tighten and loosen, as if the Jack weren't dead but breathing and undulating still. He'd skinned it and sawed the carcass in two; he was working on the left half now. In the morning, a small army of helpers would arrive, aid his quest to make the beast not only palatable, but downright delicious. Christy would make her stew from the chuck, and Brandy would help him with the blood sausage. He just needed to get everything properly sliced and diced and prepped, sectioned off and accessible to the cooks coming by. He'd oversee and manage the rollout of the Jack feast, but his real duty—the butchery and reduction of the beast—would be over, and he'd be able to sideline himself, drink coffee, pass around the Cookbook, and answer any questions that arose around the kitchen. He decided to take a quick break and walked outside the hut. The storm had come and gone, and the air was calm and still as he lit a cigarette and felt the blood on his paws tighten and loosen. He looked up at the quarter moon and nodded. He treated it like an old friend he hadn't spoken to in ages; the distance too great to produce real intimacy, he settled for neighborly acknowledgment instead. He listened to the sounds, the crickets, the frogs, and for all the annoyance, he felt good being up in the middle of the night, hacking away at some creature. He felt at one with the natural world, as if late-night butchery were integral to its overall design. He heard a howl and howled back. He nodded again to the moon and said, "Adieu," and went back inside.

84

Pam had a weird dream that night; she saw visions of Bill (recent victim and short-lived writer). He was directly in front of her, a close-up detailing a moving mouth with a hushed voice. He said that the world is strange and getting stranger. She said, "Yup," and he nodded. He told her that there was nothing she could do, and when she heard those words, her heart sank. "Nothing to do about what?" she asked. "There's nothing you can do," he repeated, "nothing you can do about any of it." He walked away and told her to follow. They wandered through the woods; a green fog followed them. They made it to a lone hut, heavily lit with neon signs. Bill held the door for Pam. Inside, she saw Jean and Jefferson shuffling down the aisles, each sampling the wares, pocketing goods, and chewing vigorously on an assortment of homemade sweets. It was a candy shack, and she saw Mandy and Sandra too, tucked far off in the corner, each with a bag, chowing down. She saw Deputy Deidra (a younger rendition of herself) and Tim Dominguez talking together, and Hymen was working the cash register. Everyone seemed to be gathered here, or many of the main players, at least. Pam went to eat a bonbon, but Bill slapped it out of her paw, and she dropped it. "That ain't for you." She was annoyed by this sudden reprimand, but Bill turned, thinking nothing of it, and kept walking to the end of the store. "Keep up now," he said.

There was another door in the back, a cheap wooden thing on rusty hinges, and Bill unlocked it with a key on a string that he'd pulled from his pocket. "This way," he said. She followed, and it was dark in there. He pulled at a cord—*light*! And the sudden reveal threw her for a loop. It was Jim, tied to a chair, head hanging forward, gagged and sweating with a bullet hole in his head.

"I told ya, there wasn't nothing you could do."

She started to cry and stroked the damp head of Jim. She kept trying to look him in the eye, as if by doing so he'd wake up, regain consciousness, and through the meeting of their gazes, he'd return to her.

He did not and remained lifeless, and she broke down in sobs beside him. When she woke up, Jim was in the bathroom putting on deodorant. He looked at her and smiled, and then he started to sing.

85

It was a beautiful day out. The sky was clear, and Jefferson was opening up the gas station for the early birds. Already grinning to himself, knowing the workday would be brief. Soon he'd be facedown at the feast, scarfing on Jack. He hoped for a steak, sides of mashed potatoes, heaping mounds of corn—braised short ribs. He knew whatever it was, it'd be well supplied; from all indicators, this Jack character was a big son of a gun. Enough feed for the whole warren... given ample sides and appetizers accompanied the beast's meat. He'd have a light breakfast, then hold off, saving himself for the big event. Liam hopped by outside, and Jefferson waved through the window. He poured himself a coffee as the door opened, and Jim and his two daughters wandered in.

"Well, if it isn't the man himself," said Jefferson.

Jim smiled and blushed, unable to hide his happiness.

"I'd sure like to shake the hand of the rabbit who killed that darn Jack."

Jim walked up and shook paws with Jefferson.

"Hi, Jefferson. You coming by the feast today?"

"Yes, sir. I'll be closing up at four and coming over afterwards. You girls excited? Your daddy's the one who put that darn Jack in the ground. You know that?"

Mandy piped up. "Yes, we're very proud."

Jim blushed again and maneuvered his daughters on. "Go grab some breakfast, girls. Mom's waiting on us."

Jim paid for the gas and the food at the till. Jefferson nodded to them and let his one ear flop down as they exited his establishment. He felt really good today. The chemicals in his brain were putting him in a wonderful mood. He popped a pill with his coffee to reinforce the behavior of his neurotransmitters; he gave them an additional boost.

86

The locksmith arrived at Bill's tree house that morning. He'd been called by Pam to repair the damaged lock from the night she and Jim had hidden in there. The locksmith moved slowly from his work truck, an overweight rabbit in overalls, swaying slightly with his motions. He gripped the planks and proceeded to climb the tree. He'd inspect the damage first before grabbing his tools. He got inside Bill's tree house and flipped the hatch down; they'd pried off the lock and busted off some of the wood. He'd do a quick patch-up job now and replace the whole thing later. He looked around the inside; he saw the words, "Make good." He noticed diagrams and pictures and words scribbled all over the place. The place piqued his curiosity; he did a lap around, and the strange pictures and drawings made the locksmith's insides tighten up and coil like a snake. He saw some pages sitting on a desk; he walked towards them. He read the following: "*When someone enters, it's no accident. They were called there. It dictates the order. It moves and shifts beneath the earth.*

Requires certain souls and directs the design of all that's above. It writes the tale. The grand author—using the peons and the blood to keep the game drifting forward. Sally Buford saw this, and then the Room ate her. Her part was played, her character no longer necessary in the yarn to come. All that happens here is dictated by her hand; the Room watches and supplies the monsters and the accolades. No one escapes her grasp, and all the guest stars have recurring roles with different faces. It's a beautiful game that I do not understand; there's cruelty and love involved, but I cannot decipher the mixture. Perhaps she's insane; I cannot tell. Her motives remain a mystery. She is the greatest dancer, and she never sleeps; she will never die..."

The locksmith didn't know what to think of that. It seemed like an odd bit of writing; a paragraph of rubbish—but he'd read it, and perhaps that meant something. He came in and that grouping of words waited for him on the page to approach. It was a lingering trap that he'd fallen right into. He closed the hatch and descended the tree. The day was almost done. The feast would soon begin.

87

Tim was in the foyer of Curtis' cave waiting on his uncle. He was nervous about the feast for some reason. He could feel himself tighten up and was so weirdly bent out of shape by all the events and the sudden conclusion of Jack that all he knew was that he wanted to get there as soon as he could. He cared little for the actual fact that he was to eat the beast, somehow that even seemed wrong. But he wanted to see what was next for him, and somehow the feast represented the next chapter. Curtis was taking his time, had unearthed an old grey suit that he was still fumbling with, unable to get the tie to lie at the proper length. He exited his bedroom and met Tim at the entrance, his tie comically short. Tim let out a slight laugh and helped his uncle, retying the tie one final time.

They hopped in the SUV and drove towards Pickmore Park. It was only a little after 2 p.m., but Curtis could tell Tim wanted to get out there; they'd presumably be one of the first to arrive, but that was fine. They'd have first pick at a good spot, a seat near the action. Curtis guessed that a performance or two would be organized. A local band or a children's choir, or maybe a play... like the ones Ms. Duvroy used to put on during certain choice events with a ragtag bunch of amateur thespians. He enjoyed these spectacles. As he pulled up to Pickmore Park, he noticed Deputy Dean signaling him to the left. He rolled down his window, and the deputy greeted him amicably.

"Howdy, Curtis. Here for the feast, eh?"

"Yes, sir."

The deputy tipped his hat to Tim. "Hi, son. Well, you fellas turn in here and find yourselves a spot. Deborah and some others are just finishing up setting the tables. Enjoy, fellas."

Tim smiled at the deputy but didn't say anything. Curtis drove on and parked, and as they walked towards the site, they noticed the floral designs weaved and wrapped around the tables. The event signaled an aesthetic shift within the warren, an almost spring-like becoming, the storm from last night breaking and giving rise to a sunny afternoon dedicated to the digestion of the warren's most terrifying predator. For all involved, it seemed like a triumph, a win... except for Tim, who still felt that the battle wasn't over; the foe remained, even as they were preparing to eat it bit by bit. Somehow, the evil still lurked, its pedigree hailing back from a time before the warren even existed. He took a seat at a picnic table near the wooden amphitheater; Curtis went off to get them something to drink. One of his teachers, Mr. Headwick, came up to the table. He was dressed in a furry black costume; only his head remained as Tim remembered, poking through the bushel of pelage and smiling at him.

"How are you, Tim?" he said. "Like the costume? I'm in today's play, the titular villain in fact."

Tim smiled awkwardly, and he heard Mr. Headwick's stomach growl; the player was beginning to get very hungry.

88

Tom arrived around 4 p.m. He parked and sauntered off, waving to the deputy and hearing all the hubbub of the festivities well underway. Most of the long picnic tables were packed with families and little ones. The majority of the town had made the trip and were eager to partake and celebrate with their neighbors on such a lovely and joyous day at Pickmore Park. A play was being staged, and most people were fixated on the action. A furry black figure in a deranged mask pranced around, and a gun-toting rabbit with a bandana (played by the town's mortician) shared the stage. Tom figured he was catching the tail end of the show.

He saw Jean over with Pam and Jim up front. There wasn't any room at their table. He should have come earlier. The main area where the feast would soon appear was dressed with flowers and ornamental arrangements, and the sight of the community all gathered together made Tom feel good; he sat down at an empty seat near the back. Some unknown kid cocked his head towards him; Tom smiled, but the kid

remained unfazed, a stoic expression, no curl to his lip. Tom
turned to watch the play.

89

The play had been designed the night before by Ms. Duvroy. She'd brewed her coffee and, much like Horace, had accepted her nocturnal task—to be completed, in its entirety, in a twelve-hour stretch; thus, she'd have enough time to chat and rehearse with her four actors: Mr. Headwick (teacher), Sally Hearse (nurse), Joe Benton (mortician), and Mr. Woodhawk (unemployed). She typed well into the night; having done such rushed jobs a time or two before, she knew to work in broad strokes, toss as much color at the canvas as it'd allow. Then she'd pare it down if need be. Her actors were used to such short schedules and a lack of rehearsals, although they'd have certainly appreciated some time to hone their characters, perfect their cadence, whet their moves. Improvisation played an integral role in their performance, just as it did in Ms. Duvroy's penning of the play. She dove forward without much of a plan, kept it to a ten-page maximum, wrote specifically for the actors she had on hand, knowing their weaknesses of character and the strength in their convictions; she used the gossip funneling out of the warren and the newscasts and her telephone to inspire her, send her in offbeat directions all the while adhering to the short gestation period her play allowed, *never looking back, always pushing forward*. It was a nascent piece of writing, soon to be performed for the eyes of the warren. She called it *The Death of Jack* (for simplicity's sake) but used the working title *The Burr in the Fur*—a title she preferred—when referencing it with the cast.

The play was nearing its conclusion, and the audience seemed thoroughly engaged. Ms. Duvroy mouthed the words as Joe Benton articulated them to the crowd. "Now die, you big sombitch!" The mortician raised his mock gun at Mr. Headwick; he pulled the trigger, and a boom went off. Mr. Headwick performed a harrowing death for the rabbits to witness. He danced and clenched his faux wound and crumpled to the floor. The mortician raised his gun and planted one foot on the deceased Jack, articulating a gesture of victory as the crowd applauded and hooted and hollered, and little Jimmy Brooks, who'd guzzled too much milk (too captivated by the madness of the show to focus on the pleas of his organs), bent over and puked near the side of his table. Mrs. McRoy turned and watched the whole event as milk poured forth from his little rabbit nose.

90

Horace watched as the meal was entering its final phase of completion. Garnishes were being added, and the lineup of eats provided by the Jack was something to behold. He was quite impressed with both his own doings and those of his army of cooks. A variety of dishes and stews and sausages and roasts were displayed on gold-tinted trays, some of which were hand-painted with floral designs. Beakers of gravy and au jus were lined up, ready to be taken to the main stage for their distribution to the warren. Appetites were sky-high, and Horace salivated, sampling a bit of the pulled shoulder they'd braised since dawn. It tasted so goddamn good he forgot himself and kissed Jolene Wilds on the cheek as she sprinkled parsley over the potato salad. "Good?" she asked, slightly flustered.

"Goddamn delicious," said Horace.

His eyes were strange, debauched somehow. Jolene supposed it was because of the approaching end, a euphoric eruption because of the completed task—worry and stress leading straight to pleasure and weightlessness. But this wasn't it; deep inside of Horace, the Jack was breaking down, amalgamating, overturning his gastral harmony, and corrupting him from the inside out. It was all coming to a head. It was all part of the plan. The Jack would have its revenge; it was the art of war and sacrifice and digestion, and it was all concealed by a cloak of deliciousness.

91

Doc was nearing some big event in his story. The dwarf clown had proved a worthy character, navigating the curves of the narrative and scheming his way to the top of the town's social hierarchy with little trouble. He'd killed the clown in the woods and taken up its face, had charmed the townsfolk, bedded a few beauties, gambled and won an assortment of riches, and here he was, standing a smidge over four feet tall, ready to put the final wheel in motion and watch the events play out of their own accord. It was time for him to step back and watch the carefully placed dominos tumble; the orchestration had taken time, but the fall would be worth it—soon it would commence, and the maelstrom would once again reign.

Doc wiped a bit of liquid near his eye; he couldn't tell whether it was a tear or sweat or blood. He accepted the secretions as they came out, thinking of them as one and the same. His body's nectar leaking out for one purpose or another. He was pushing forward without any thoughts outside of what was being written before him. The Room kept him focused and pleased, and above her, at the other end of town, the first table of picnicking rabbits went up to the feast and began to fill their plates.

92

Sheriff Huckston was the first to notice it. Along with the other rabbits, he'd dug in. He'd already put one heaping plate away, devouring it in no time. Jack's juice leaked down from his chin, leftover liquid from a dazzling filet mignon. He was putting away creamed corn mixed with his mashed potatoes, shoveling it at an excessive pace. The cooks had outdone themselves. He saw Horace standing near the main table, carving prime rib for a lineup of eager rabbits. All sounds and information seemed lost to him; the spell of the feast accentuated the reach of his taste buds and ordained them the guiding voice of his vessel. He stared ahead, forgetting Richard and Willard and the deputies; for they too were hunkered down, all focus dedicated to the task at hand. It was a slight rumbling in his gut that told Sheriff Huckston that something wasn't quite right. He burped and looked up with a puzzled expression on his face. It was as if he was shot with a bullet and knew it was all too late. He panned across the crowd and watched how everyone was eating. The Jack distributed liberally among the community, forkfuls of flavor and tissue being devoured by the little rabbits. And then he saw it through the shadows of the trees, a colossal being pushing through the forest. The sheriff tried to speak, warn those at his table, but the mouthful of corn and potatoes proved difficult to maneuver his tongue around. Food flopped out of Sheriff Huckston's mouth as he tried to yell, "Monster!"

93

But it wasn't a monster, at least not one that any of the other rabbits could yet see. For them, the shock on the sheriff's face (along with his quasi-scream) made little impression; they were lost in the frivolities of the feast. Richard puzzled over it for a brief moment before returning to his liver stew; a wide-eyed sheriff could be accounted for by many things... perhaps he'd seen a long-lost girlfriend wander past. Richard scooped up another forkful and left the sheriff to gaze up, mumbling, unconcerned by the terror on his face, but it wasn't long before a growing sense of unease spread across the picnic tables, traveling from rabbit to rabbit. Richard looked at Willard and saw that his solemn and dependable partner wore a grimace unlike any he'd ever fashioned before; it hovered between fear and apprehension and disgust (with a pinch of anticipation). Richard asked if he was all right, and Willard said, "Uh-oh." That was all, but it was enough to nudge Richard out of his comfort and brace for the ensuing impact of what was soon to be.

Willard looked at Richard, and the rabbit's face melted away; a skeleton with two furry ears stared back at him from the darkness of two black orbits.

"Are you all right?" asked Richard the skeleton.

Willard couldn't suffer the pain of articulating what he was suddenly seeing. He looked down, and the space beneath him shifted. A blackness sifted out of everything now—a strange form of X-ray vision colored the bones around him in a fluorescent green glow. His eyesight orchestrated around a new set of rules, and he watched as a picnic of bones settled around a nightly scene. Dust-like molecules radiating light drifted through the forest. A temporal shift had claimed the warren—or, at least, that's what Willard first thought. Explanations regarding the sudden visual shift left his lips mute while his mind plodded on in painful disarray. He said, "Bones," and he looked at Sheriff Huckston; his skeleton had fallen over and made a mad dash into the woods. Soon the others, too, were screaming, a mass of rabbits in the grips of a psychotic breakdown. The blood of Jack pulled and tightened and loosened in their insides, and their faculties waned and waxed as their sanity crumbled, and their hallucinations dictated the rules of the game.

94

Pam couldn't see at all. Her reaction had been blindness—the world closed its shutters and remained void to her now. She called out for her daughters and Jim, and in return, she heard nothing. It was as if her senses had faltered, filtering out all the information, all the hysteria, and in some ways, it seemed worse. She was excluded from the fight, lost and unable to return to the loved ones who, moments before, were sitting right next to her. The Jack inside of her had switched off her most basic means of communicating with the world—blind and deaf, she called out and stumbled along; she'd tried to sit and calm herself, chant the names of those nearest and dearest to her, but someone or something had run into her (a blunt blow to the head); it took her a minute to steady herself, and once she did, she felt it necessary to continue on, hoping that she could navigate according to a handful of vivid memories of Pickmore Park, maneuver out of harm's way. She felt what she supposed were trees and leaned up against one; she'd traveled a small distance, and she wanted to remove herself from the mess, but not so far that Jim and the girls couldn't find her. *What had they eaten?* she thought. *What was the Jack doing to everyone's insides?* The warren was in a crisis of food poisoning, and how long would its effects last? Or was this simply the beginning of the end?

Pam crouched with her back against a tree. She tried to hum to herself in the hopes that she could hear her own rumblings. She remained deaf and huddled. Jefferson saw her; he was bleeding from his head, and his eyes were unfocused. "You all right, Pam?" She didn't reply, and so he kept on. He stumbled until he came to a giant crater in the earth. It had never been there before, but this seemed unimportant. He climbed down, wobbly and goofy-footed—onward and upward, or, in this case, down and spellbound. He winded along a circular path, twisting around the hole. Structures emerged, broken ruins of old shelters—a secret society living beneath the warren. He poked his head into a building with a crumbling roof. A portrait of an old rabbit, dust-covered and decaying, hung on one of the remaining stone walls. He kept downward, and the path kept going. He knew he should return, go see to his store, reopen for the community, fuel up his fellow rabbits—but something pushed him to continue along his downward trek. Some immense pressure crushed the rational modes of thought dictating the decisions of his journey. He needed to discover this place that had—until recently—been hidden and deteriorating beneath his feet, swallowed whole and digested as he worked (ignorant of its existence) on the solid terrain above. He saw another house, this one simply a lone freestanding stone wall arching above a fireplace. A cauldron, half buried in the dirt, lay among the remains. He began to unearth it, scooping out handfuls of earth and carving out around its submerged section. He pulled at the handle, and it came away. He felt like that was enough for one day, and he packed up his cauldron and headed back to see what had become of the rabbits above.

95

As Jefferson made his way back to the picnic tables of Pickmore Park, he saw an assortment of images—vague and unreal and drifting—and he was unable to make sense of it. Rabbits ran, screamed, giggled; some were crouched over others; blood pooled around some lying prostrate in the dirt. He clutched his cauldron and carried on. He looked at the sun and watched as it split in two. He put the cauldron down and began to add ingredients into its mix. He scoured the tables for bits of food and tossed in a rogue ear from some unknown rabbit that he'd found bloodied and freshly torn on the ground. He seemed unbothered by the activities of the others, by their violence—he worked methodically on his potion. He found a fire not far and put his cauldron near it, allowing its contents to come to a boil. He simmered his stew and tasted his creation, and beside him, a pair of rabbit's feet lay still; the rest of it, scorched and burned, lay inside the fire.

"She started with a good sentence, then followed it. For it was a brand of piecemeal decimation. *It was her art of war.*"

Jefferson heard one of the rabbits say this (almost in a whisper), but it barely registered as he took a spoonful of his mixture and swallowed the spell.

96

Tom had somehow gotten home to his apartment; he had no memory of this. He was at the festival, saw snippets of horror erupt—rabbit-on-rabbit violence, full-blown madness enveloping the warren. Rabbits cried and screamed and laughed; some were certainly dead. And then somehow, unbeknownst to him, he'd made it safe and sound back to his lodging. He listened to hear if Pam or Jim or the girls had made it home, but he didn't hear a damn thing. He was still twisted in the mind, and he caught himself staring dumbly at the bathroom tiles for minutes on end. He felt his guts bellow and moan, and he scrambled to the toilet, shitting at a furious pace. He yelped as he evacuated the waste. Eating that Jack (although a supposedly longstanding tradition among the warren, documented throughout its history and literature) had proven to be an unwelcome event in a continuous lineup of senseless tragedy. He wondered momentarily if it was all over now, but he knew that the devil was apt to raise the pitch and heighten the frequency at any moment. *What are the limits of horror?* he thought to himself. Perhaps they defy logic and are constantly reborn and renewed. An unwinding of all that is beautiful and tethered; the links that have become the foundation for a life—the putrefaction... of love and neighborly affection and friendships and kinky passion. A chewing away, and a reformation towards the husk form. An erosion and crumbling of the interior. A sturdy home with nothing inside.

Tom turned on the TV and watched the light pulse and flicker at his pupils. He sat inches away and tried to push his head into the portal beaming inward from this strange device. His phone rang, and it spooked him, and his head hit the screen. He sprang into action and grabbed it from the receiver.

"Hello?"

He could hear heavy breathing.

"Outside..." said the voice.

He dashed for the window and looked down. He saw Pam on her cellular staring up at him. She raised a hand and offered a strange wave. He buttoned his coat and left straight away; his apartment remained unlocked.

97

Tim had not eaten the Jack. The sight of the beast neatly placed and lopped apart into an assortment of dishes and cuisines left him feeling mildly nauseous. He'd watched his uncle eat at a furious speed, chuckling and scooping Jack up in tiny mouthfuls as he joked and nodded to the rabbits sitting across from them. He was late to succumb to the hallucinations and gastric malice of the Jack. Tim had watched as the tables of rabbits had begun to act strangely, some yelling, others running right into the woods, and still some (like Uncle Curtis) who sat immobile, lost in the caverns of their own minds. He'd sensed something wrong and had tried to help those scattered at random around Pickmore Park, but then the violence had started. Old man Harry had bludgeoned his former school pal Derek with a shovel and bashed his head in, only to sit and pluck small daffodils from the forest floor and plant them in the cracked skull of his friend. Tim tried to move his uncle, but Curtis remained mute and unwilling to budge, pushing Tim away after one concerted effort that'd proved worthless. Tim, feeling remiss, left toward his uncle's cave. *Let the warren sort out its own insanity,* he'd decided, *or succumb to it, for that matter.* Whichever way, he'd come back once the Jack had run its course through the anatomy of the warren. See who was left standing once all was said and done. He crossed his fingers that Uncle Curtis would be all right. But only time would tell.

98

Life had become a twisted story where his favorite characters were apt to die out. Tom wasn't sure who was all right and who was dead, but he was happy to see Pam. When he'd first approached her down in the trees below their tenement, she'd doubled over and puked, and then she'd looked at him and said, "Once I was blind, but now I can see." She seemed far worse than he was. He asked where Jim and the girls were, and she shrugged; she started to dance and move back into the forest. Tom followed her. They continued this way; she seemed euphoric and mad. Tom too was fighting with this fever and, once or twice, had to swallow the bile pumping up into his mouth. He found himself back at Pickmore Park. It was nightfall, and some tables had been thrown together and lit on fire. Rabbits lay scattered around, mostly the remains of those unlucky enough to fall victim to the Jack in their guts or the surrounding hysteria of their neighbors. Tom navigated through moments of lucidity and looked to see who was dead. He found Jean facedown, not breathing. Peter

Downborough, a co-worker of Tom's, was decapitated, and deep in the back was Jim. His arm was bent sideways and sticking straight up from the dirt in such a way as to signal a colloquial (if not grotesque) wave. Tom approached and could see plainly that he was dead, mud coated all over his face and body; Tom stared at Jim for a long while as Pam danced about. The body of Jim lay still, grinning up at him.

99

Doc continued his tale of the dwarf clown and watched as his creation (or the Room's creation summoned through him) took a detour, and the dwarf clown, the entity of power and virility, relinquished its hold over the town it had come to claim. Slowly but surely, he watched as the machinations of his plan played out and then amalgamated into the collective psyche of the town and its surviving inhabitants. Dawn had broken in his story and, along with it, the spell that the dwarf clown had cast. The map had been reconfigured throughout his meddling, and now he left the inhabitants to fend for themselves in a new post-calamity era. What would they do now to whittle away the hours? Were they so broken and beyond the bounds of repair that this next chapter would spark a divergent trajectory? Or would everything resume much like before? The town would soon decide for itself, reveal its hand from the freshly dealt deck.

It was at this point in his writing that Doc decided to take a break. He lit a cigarette. He noticed the overheard light again, and he stared up at it.

He was beginning to believe that God did exist. He was the accumulations of all the ghosts in all the machines, and He had a nefarious and dumb sense of humor.

100

Sandra and Mandy were far into the woods. Mandy was crying; her sister, bamboozled out of her brains, did her best to keep them moving; that's all she knew how to do. The warren had gone mad, and they too had developed the sickness. Sandra had seen visions of a godlike beast manufacture itself out of a small fire that soon swept up the entire scene, only to have the monster disappear in a flash and transfigure itself into two shapely squirrels sprinting up a tree. Moments of lucidity revealed treacherous violence on behalf of the warren, destroying its own kind under the directives of a malevolent gastric entity. Their fallen foe had pulled the wool over their eyes, and its destructive tendencies persisted even after its death. The Jack had demonstrated a cunning and Machiavellian twist, an evolutionary adjustment that dealt its final blow at the moment when the warren was relaxed and placated. It was no wonder they had fallen so hard. Their vigilance had been at an all-time low.

101

Jefferson was still out of his mind while the rest of the warren had fallen over, gone comatose for the betterment of their body, given time to flush the poison from the machine. Jefferson, on the other hand, had continued to concoct a whole arrangement of chow in his cauldron that he kept ingesting and offering to those few around him who seemed sensible enough to interact with and were still somehow on their feet. Deputy Deidra had cuffed him across the face when he'd approached her with a ladle of his stew. He'd tumbled backwards, tripping over the corpse of some unknown fellow. He watched her as she walked past and knelt beside Loralie who lay dead or unconscious on the ground. She held her paw and began to weep. Jefferson carried on as the sun began to peek through the trees. Stirring and stirring, he sipped small mouthfuls while seated in the lotus position.

He noticed movement and agitation as some of the rabbits on the ground began to rise up. Hangovers of an unfathomable variety would be handed out to the survivors who were lucky enough to wake from last evening's nightmares. He would offer them a scoopful of his concoction. *Hair of the dog that bit ya*, he thought.

102

Richard had come around. He stood up, aloof and in pain. He gripped his head and tried to massage his temples. He stood around Willard, who'd written, "It's all part of the plan," in the dirt surrounding his body. He was dead, sacrificed in some ritualistic death dance brought on by a blade, fancifully displaying his intestines in an outrageous cursive manner. He was an adept hand with a knife, and his artistry was on full display. Richard stifled a gagging fit; his head ached, and he sat down lonesome on the ground near his disemboweled *compañero*; unable to find solace even in grief, he started to cry—more out of a common frustration than anything else. The pain in his head was mounting, and his gags were beginning to break through; the throw-up was coming. He knelt beside his friend and read the words again. *It's all part of the plan.* He envisioned himself taking a note from Willard's book and performing his own brand of seppuku. Two suicides gone to waste out in the woods—defeated by the decadence of the feast. He puked and felt better; his wits were slowly coming back. He crawled off further into the forest and passed out under a harsh ray of sunlight.

103

Sandra and Mandy had wandered their way past Mission Heights. They'd curved up a hillside entrance and come to a yard with an assortment of children playing and frolicking out front. Mandy recognized one of the kids, Samantha Wentworth.

She said: "Are you alright?"

And Samantha responded: "Yes."

She kept playing. Each Wentworth kid seemed to be out on the lawn, each inhabiting their own make-believe world. They seemed normal enough.

"Were you at the feast?" asked Sandra, her hands trembling slightly from the pain and weakness of processing the Jack.

"No, we weren't allowed."

Samantha barely looked up at them; she kept her eyes focused on her doll. A cat came out from a bush and hissed at the sisters before circling Samantha and then re-entering the hole it'd first burst forth from.

"It's a hot day today," said Samantha.

"Yup," said Sandra Kurtz.

The sisters kept on; they moseyed through the woods, sampled wild strawberries that they'd found along their route and drank from a spring. Samantha had been right, and the day was going to be a hot one. Their youth had given them an upper hand as far as the Jack was concerned, and their bodies had turned a corner and were restabilizing after the psychoactive meat of the monster. Mandy wondered if there would be any long-term complications, would she re-enter that state at random intervals, forever destined to return to that hell now that her innards had been scarred by the Jack. The wind picked up, offering a cooling breeze as the sisters marched on.

"Should we go home?" asked Mandy.

Sandra didn't answer her directly and simply bade her to come on.

In the midst of their trying night, Mandy remembered that for the briefest of moments, she'd looked up and thought the world had caught fire, and in that recollection, she recalled a moment of unbridled beauty.

104

Tom and Pam had lingered at Pickmore Park. Pam's brain was recalibrating the landscape, and her usual manner of interpreting the world was slowly coming back into the fold. Her insanity hadn't been entirely washed away, but slowly feelings of a more rational nature were pushing in (soon sensible reasoning would follow suit, tender a tangible reading of the terrain). She felt that something was wrong, the euphoria and the haze that had dictated her directions throughout the night, a confident and chaotic energy, were winding down, no longer virile and potent with strands of lunacy—but dull and bankrupt and without any bite. She stared at the bodies stranded in the dirt; she had yet to identify Jim. Tom had made the rounds and took a count of all the deceased. It seemed to him that roughly a third of the attendees had perished during the soirée. A substantial decrease in the warren's population had occurred in a single night. Death had come down in many forms. Each rabbit seemed to have succumbed in a wholly fitting manner particular to their personality type. Some folk (of a more modest bent) had died without any outward show of theatrics, simply tumbling over, eyes open, transfixed by some distant and far-off event; some wore grins—most wore neutral expressions. Tom classified these casualties as type A. The type Bs were different; they were the Willards of the lot, the ones who'd committed violence against themselves in a variety of ways: the suicides. Tom figured that those of a more introspective nature (even if outwardly he might have classified them as extroverts) were the sort who'd fallen under the banner of the Bs. Type C was a different animal altogether. The victims of those who'd transgressed and adopted the role of murderer were grouped here. All the murderees—whether choked, bashed, broken down, cut up, dismembered, or reconfigured—belonged here. It seemed unlikely, but from Tom's count, all three types were more or less distributed evenly among the dead. An equal partitioning of violence. Tom watched Jefferson through the trees. He was a hundred or so yards away with his back turned, sampling his stew from his cauldron, still ladling his tonic up to his mouth, one mouthful at a time.

105

Deputy Deidra was still holding Loralie's hand. Loralie had perished during the night, and now that the deputy's mind was coming back around, she started to feel the gnawing attack of grief cripple her core. Her only defense so far had been the pain in her head, her atrocious hangover which had butted in, bullying her focus, dulling Loralie's death. But the physical torment was subsiding, and the full heft of the emotional burden would soon take hold. She looked up and saw Sheriff Huckston sitting on a picnic table; his head turned downward, cupped in his paws. There would be a massive burial and songs and kind words; she knew that. Another community affair to punctuate the ending of this disastrous one.

Deputy Dean walked up to her. "Arleen's dead."

Deputy Deidra didn't say anything.

"Are you alright?" asked the deputy.

The best she could communicate was a gravelly burst from her throat. She wasn't sure what she was trying to communicate with it apart from a shared series of sounds that she figured Deputy Dean was expecting.

"I'm gonna go check on the sheriff," he said.

She didn't try to make any more sounds. She held Loralie's paw and was happy to be left alone again. In the distance, she saw two vehicles park. A shocked group of rabbits got out and entered Pickmore Park. Wide-eyed with mouths open, they walked past and surveyed the grounds. Deputy Deidra refocused her attention on Loralie; she kissed her paw and got up and walked off alone. The birds were chirping loudly. She rubbed her face with slumped shoulders and carried on. She craved her bed and a sinking into bottomless sleep.

106

Some days have passed, and the warren is still coming to terms with the events out at Pickmore Park. All survivors were supposed to rendezvous at the hospital for a checkup, determine that the danger they had faced was no longer a concern. A preliminary medical examination that, for some, marked the beginning of a new chapter in which their anatomy had been altered and bent—enlarged kidneys, scarring of the lungs and heart—things that needed to be taken into account, recorded and investigated, dealt with by a series of appointments and carefully monitored tests.

A mass of funerals had been organized, graves dug, hymns sung, the rabbits all dressed in their finest threads to pay their respects to the loved ones, neighbors, friends, cohorts, and acquaintances they'd lost. Those who'd committed crimes were all acquitted, except for a rabbit named Jeremiah who'd snuffed out six rabbits while hopped up on the Jack. A year before during a drunken night out, he'd run over a rabbit, Chrissy Acorn, killing her instantly. Jeremiah was sent to the gallows. He was hung under the watchful eye of Sheriff Huckston, Deputy Deidra, and the medical examiner. His final words were: "Why me?"

During a town meeting, a vote was taken and a new development was approved for Pickmore Park. The park was set to be demolished and rebuilt as a memorial site to honor those who'd succumbed during the Jack attack and the subsequent feast. A statue would be erected and a series of benches added with the names of those who'd fallen etched into plaques adorning the backrests. A local artist named Jonathan Tusselsmith was commissioned for both the benches and the statue. He was more or less a recluse, and of the few occasions when he'd left his workshop, out at Patty's Diner (a brief window of time away from his travails, allowing his subconscious to bear the brunt of the load—crafting a multitude of possible scenarios—as his conscious mind bumbled on), the other rabbits chided him about being so gosh darn tight-mouthed, asking him and pleading for a photo or, at the very least, a detailed description of the work. Jonathan never caved to his neighbors' appeals. He toiled and worked for three months on his creation in utter secrecy before it was presented to the judgment and curiosity of the public eye.

During the unveiling, a storm had snuck up. Dark clouds had blotted out periwinkle skies, and a large number of the warren had turned up bearing thermoses and umbrellas. Unruly weather could not stamp out their participation in the event that some hoped would put an end—and thus add closure—to the whole Jack fiasco. It was a show of respect to the dead, to their brethren. A large taupe covering hung limp around the statue as the warren stared up at the mysterious monument. The benches were already on display and were met with universal acclaim; many rabbits had already taken their seat on them, choosing one after carefully inspecting the names etched into the design. Jonathan was near the statue, talking with Maureen Redhorn, the town elder. She was there as a formality, the oldest and wisest rabbit of the lot who was asked to remove the covering and thus display the statue in its rightful place for the first time. She had two long scars running across her face, and her movements were slow and her manner was taciturn. She walked with a cane fashioned from a branch of a maple tree, and when the rabbits of the warren talked to her, her response was typically a smile, broadening across her face, as she looked up to meet their gaze. Very rarely was any advice administered in words; her smiles displayed the alchemy of her answers. Some rabbits thought she was a genius—while others thought she was a fool. It was one of the more popular topics of discussion in the warren. Generally, the consensus was on the side of the fool, but she had her admirers and devotees, and they were a fervent bunch.

When Maureen pulled the tarp to reveal the statue, Jonathan stood right next to her; his veneer remained calm. The tarp came loose with one jerky tug, and the warren gasped as they looked up at his marble creation. It was a whirlwind of action swirling together, a Gothic piece high-lighting the event as a multitude of rabbits were morphing into one another around its outer fringes. In the center stood an erect Jack, fierce and defiant, some rabbits were attacking him with axes, and the moment depicted (although fan-tastical) was nonetheless a moving representation of the horror and bravery of the rabbits facing down their foe (even if it was somewhat out of tune with the cold, hard facts). Applause and hoots and cheers sounded off. Jonathan took a bow as Maureen smiled broadly at him and then aimed her grin at the other rabbits as she panned her head from left to right. In the back, Jefferson stood leaning against a tree. His one ear flopped to the side. He didn't make any sounds but kept staring at the statue. To him, it looked different. It had a winding appeal, like a tornado, or a face... like the one that man had had... disfigured and wrapped in wire. He stared with a blank look, and he mumbled some gibberish.

The cock in the wire,
Cooked in the fire,
Emerges changed,
Airs its game.

107

When Doc had stepped out of the Room, he found himself at the other end of the warren. A remote area, miles away from Bill's bunker. He could have sworn it was the same door he'd used to enter into the Room—the tight, tunneling corridor in Bill's workshop—but this was not so. Or perhaps the Room had made some alterations during his time within it. He'd concluded his tale of the dwarf clown. His hands had emerged ragged and bloody from the machine's constant pecking. With his manuscript complete, piled high on the table next to his ashtray, he'd felt the Room direct his attention—and he saw, to his left, a large chalice atop a slender pillar roughly fifty feet away. He picked up his manuscript and walked over to it. There was a pack of matches lying next to the chalice, and he lit one of the matches and touched its flame to the lip of the cup. It took light; its mouth expanded, and its dimensions began to alter. He stared at it and then placed his manuscript inside the enlarged cup and watched it burn as ash drifted up and pieces of burning paper floated by and around the Room. He felt directed again. He walked up to another table, slow and lethargic, as if the required effort was huge or simply that time was no longer a concern. A latex mask was lying on it. A mask depicting a face not unlike his own before that fateful night out with Bill. He placed it over his head, his eyes peering through layers of vizards and wire. And then he saw the door and grabbed its handle; he shoved it open and was blinded, and his pupillary light reflex constricted his pupil to account for the newfound luminosity. He walked out into the forest once more and was delighted by the sweet smells and the light breeze. He felt good being in his old skin again.

108

Jefferson was refilling the coffee, making a fresh pot before lunch for the workers who'd be arriving soon. The routine of customers returning to his gas station at certain times, repeated intervals through the weeks and months, kept him content and structured nowadays—particularly in his current state of mind (post-Jack), still not completely out of the woods, so to speak, but working towards a more common and peaceful state of mind. His intake and consumption of the Jack had been on another level than the rest of the warren, and yet, despite his massive comedown from his intoxicated state (a stint in the hospital that had proved both horrendous and hallucinatory), there seemed to be little or few lingering effects (minus the odd flashback), and his day-to-day lifestyle was much like it'd once been. He seemed to drift off more, was less inclined to continue conversations that held no particular purpose or clear-cut end goal; *a strange exercise,* he thought, forcing his tongue to perform a sequence of acrobatic leaps around his mouth, the muscular organ wrestling around to bring forth a common and decipherable series of takeaway points that the other conversationalist could then respond to with their own brand of oral gymnastics. The tongue and the larynx and all the beautiful biology dancing together to comment on the pitch of the sun and the density of the cloud cover. He heard the door open and looked up. Doc entered and smiled at Jefferson.

"Howdy," he said.

Jefferson didn't recognize him. He smiled at his customer and asked if there was anything he needed. Doc said no, smiling all the while. Doc realized then that no one would recognize him anymore (as the madcap monster wrapped in wire), and although he'd been squarely nestled in the warren for the last few months, he was once again a stranger without any past. A newfound presence gliding into their world without any form of tarnished history. He bought a bag of chips and a coffee and exited the store. He watched Jefferson through the window as the one-eared rabbit leaned over the counter and read his tabloid magazines.

Doc walked on through the forest sipping his coffee and munching away on his snack. He wasn't entirely sure what he should do now. His purpose hadn't been spelled out for him yet. The only feeling he could intuit was that he felt like staying in this town. He hadn't the will or the drive to depart; there was still something that needed to be done, but as of yet, Doc couldn't figure out what the heck it was. He whistled as he walked and figured that in due time it'd all sort itself out.

109

The girls were watching TV as Pam prepared their lunch: tomato sandwiches with extra mayonnaise. She could hear the girls shuffling around in the living room. She looked at the mess in the sink and poured herself another cup of coffee. The doorbell rang, and Mandy yelled, "Got it!" Pam heard her run to the door, her feet sprinting across the hardwood. Pam listened and heard Tom's voice and then Mandy's giggle.

"Come in, Tom," yelled Pam from the kitchen.

He rounded the corner and popped his head through the doorway.

"Hi, Pam. How's lunch coming along?"

"Oh, you know, tasty sandwiches. You know the drill. Would you like one?"

"No thanks. I'm off to the office. I just wanted to pop in and see how y'all were doing."

"How very neighborly of you," said Pam, smiling as she lathered mayo across two slices of bread. "You can come by tonight if you like. We're ordering in, I've taxed all my culinary skills on lunch today, and the girls voted on pizza, so…"

Tom smiled and said he'd try. She kept at work as Tom fidgeted around the kitchen's entrance. He scanned its layout, caught sight of an abundance of photos stuck to the fridge. More had been added since the big event, the massive trauma. He saw Jim's face in a multitude of expressions, hugging the girls, laughing, goofing, posing with his lovely wife. After a moment of dallying, he said goodbye, waved to the girls, and made his way down to the parking garage to fetch his car and head off to work.

110

Sheriff Huckston was seated in his office. He was looking up at the clock, leaning back in his chair. The feast had set the whole department back. Deputies had been lost; friends killed off—a slew of paperwork and interviews and reports had to be completed. He was exhausted and tired in a way that he hadn't thought possible. The future had a laughable ring to it now, as if any kind of peace or happiness seemed absurd based on the evidence accrued so far; the past told him that monsters lurked damn near everywhere—especially where one was least likely to suspect them. The joy he'd once garnered from doing his job, and doing it well, was evaporating; he continued to work, diligently and efficiently, but without any emotional dividends. Something was dying inside of him, and in some strange ways, it made him a better cop. He was able to see things more clearly, but at the price of indifference, which now invaded him and forced him to float through most of his days, disconnected and hyper-rational. He could see the events and make the right calls, but he felt muddled, as if making the right or wrong decisions amounted to the same thing. Habit kept him morally sound. He heard a knock on his door and turned to see Deputy Deidra holding two coffees.

"Hey, boss."

"Howdy, Deputy."

She set the coffees down on the sheriff's desk and took a seat. "How you feeling, Sheriff?"

He smiled. "Top notch, thanks. How are you?"

111

Pam dozed off in her chair as the girls played in the living room. It was 8 a.m., and she felt herself being carried off, shuttled elsewhere in a boat, moving along choppy waters from one island to the next. And in her dream, she saw Sally Buford, and Sally asked her if she knew what'd happened— why all these events had suddenly occurred in the warren and to her and to the girls and Jim. Pam said no. Sally was seated in a warehouse it seemed. Only bits of her were lit and much of the rabbit remained hidden amongst the darkness. And Sally said, "It's about food and digestion and harmony and time. All the events—the Jack, the feast, the Room, the day-to-day monotony of it all—are part of the ecosystem you inhabit, the Great Machine. The Room dictated the need, just like it had in my time, and thus, it ate. The events themselves always seem to play out slightly out of order, a shuffled deck dealt and recalibrated but amounting to the same conclusion once all the cards were flipped. Chronology changed, but the endgame did not. Death and decomposition were integral to renewal. And thus, with the help of Jack, the warren had appeased the Room who now stood full and slumbering, gorged and momentarily off-limits, a simple organ in a larger design whose only goal was to signal the necessity of blood, lubricate the channels, and begin to satiate the salivating machine who craved meat and sacrifice. An introduction was necessary beforehand, someone would need to come knocking, rouse the Room once more, discover the constantly shifting door. Their timeline and the Room's would need to match up, the planets aligned and the stars holding in just such a way. But inevitably, these prerequisites would be met—the world was always in balance even when it wasn't—and the Room would once again send out and ensnare captives as it cultivated a plan and, in its madness, orchestrated a series of spectacular events always ending in butchery and quietus."

Pam woke up suddenly. Mandy was staring at her.

"What's wrong, honey?"

"There's a fire."

She pointed to the window, and Pam got up. She saw smoke in the distance. Pam turned on the TV and was told to stay tuned. The fire was still out of control, and the wind was picking up.

112

Tim was sitting at the table as Uncle Curtis lounged on the couch. Uncle Curtis had the TV on, watching as another eventful day played out in the warren. The fire had started in a field near Abbot Avenue and was coming closer and closer to Delaware Street where a bunch of tenements and condominiums had been set up. The news showed the firefighters and volunteers trying to extinguish the flames or hinder their progress. There was a gully from an old creek bed that held the promise of halting the fire's advances. Time would tell. Tim ate his cereal and was unbothered by the new disaster. So many tragedies had surfaced in such a short amount of time that he no longer viewed them with anything other than a detached curiosity. Uncle Curtis was all ears though, plugged into the programming as the fire worked its way towards him outside.

It was a school day for Tim, but because of the event, he figured he'd be able to play hooky and have a day to himself. Uncle Curtis would be captivated by the TV, on the phone

with his pals as the newfound drama wrapped them up—
perhaps they'd even venture out there, offer a hand at
fighting the flames. Tim told his uncle he was heading out,
and he heard him mumble a "be careful" and a "see you soon"
before he exited the door.

He marched along the well-worn path outside of Uncle
Curtis' cave. He saw a crow perched on a branch. It cawed and
cooed and rattled and clicked. He eyed it warily and kept on.

113

Sheriff Huckston had seen how the fire had started; he'd been out in his patrol car. He'd pulled over and was eating his breakfast from Judy's Diner. It was nearing sunup. He unwrapped his sandwich and was sampling the chips when he saw two young rabbits emerge from a path not far. Sheriff Huckston had seen them before, although he couldn't remember their names. He watched them as he took another bite, and Judy's secret sauce spilled out on his uniform. They were horsing around, two young males, shoving and carelessly moving along the path. Laughter and sudden jolts and cries pulled at the sheriff's attention as he did his best to mop up the mess he was making of himself; a tomato flopped down carelessly and landed on his trouser leg. One of the youngsters was smoking, and Sheriff Huckston watched as he tossed his cigarette into the bush and carried on. It was minutes later, as the sheriff was finishing up his chips and washing them down with a quenching Coke, that he saw the smoke begin to rise from a small mound of overgrown grass.

He didn't move and sipped his drink. He watched it with an air of detachment, as if the smoke were a precursor to some newfound entity making its way into the warren. He thought of those cheaply made sci-fi movies he used to watch as a kid with puffs of smoke appearing once a character had suddenly materialized or disappeared. He waited to see who was coming. The smoke gave way to flames. He drank and watched and waited.

114

Tyrone had come to the warren. He was Pete's cousin (the turtle from before). He'd heard about Pete, what had happened, and he wanted to come to the warren and investigate for himself—see what was going on with the rabbits and see how all their recent tomfoolery was playing out. He'd walked his way here, in no mood for the efficiency of modern transportation. It'd taken him a while, but there was no need to rush. He'd picked mushrooms as he journeyed his way through the forest, spent a week here and there in a variety of villages, chatted with the few folks he'd come across (although travelers were rather sparse along the route); he generally enjoyed his journey east.

The warren was quiet when he arrived, and he could smell the smoke in the air. He walked over to Jefferson's gas station, and the one-eared rabbit gave him his customary salutation.

"Good mornin', sir. How are you today?"

Tyrone nodded to the rabbit. "Very well indeed. Say, how are things going these days? I heard y'all had some Jack troubles not too far back."

Jefferson recounted the tale he'd now told countless times to newcomers and passersby; he'd quip that the monster had finally come knocking, that the warren had faced its darkest hour and come out victorious. He embellished his tale as any fine storyteller would, combining the best bits from others' accounts and combing over it to provide the best version he thought possible. Jefferson settled into his story as Tyrone stood listening.

"Was there a turtle that happened to come across this Jack?"

"I do believe there was. He was eaten from what I understand, along with a young rabbit named Kristen. An absolute tragedy, I tell you. Thank heavens the whole thing is over."

Tyrone nodded.

Tim pushed the door open; he was mindlessly playing with Dorothy's toy, flicking the pink propeller in his pocket. It'd become his good-luck piece. He halted as he saw Tyrone, surprised by the appearance of the turtle; he nodded and waved to Jefferson. He walked to the back to fish out a beverage from the refrigerator.

"Hey, Tim."

Tim turned to face Jefferson.

"Did you know Kristen?"

"Only a bit from school," he said.

Jefferson returned his attention to Tyrone and kept gabbing away. But suddenly, the world altered... the lights dimmed, and Jefferson saw Tyrone turn blue and shift like a phantasm, all smoke and hocus-pocus. He shook his head violently, tried to shake the crazy away and return to the land of normalcy. Tyrone asked if he was all right, and Jefferson explained his predicament and his newfound mental condition—brought on by a giant dose of the Jack. Things were liable to get very strange for Jefferson right out of the blue nowadays; there was no hiding from the world's wackiness; he was forced now to face it head-on, quirks and warts and all.

Tyrone thanked him for his time and bought a pack of cigarettes. He waved to Tim as he exited the door, and Tim spun the propeller and went up to pay for his drink.

115

Tom had gone out to the fire. He suddenly felt that his role was to help in any way he could. The urban planner donned a flannel sweater and was digging trenches with some other rabbits. They were increasing the range and depth of the old creek bed, hoping that this additional obstacle would be enough to halt the flames. Deputy Deidra was in charge of their sector, and she praised the rabbits' work ethic as they sweated and gulped coffee and ate donuts brought out by Deborah Brownshaw. The smoke was getting worse, and masks were handed out as the rabbits kept at work and tried their best to continue as visibility neared zero. Deputy Deidra blew an airhorn and ordered the rabbits to stop digging. That was it; time to wander home, hope that their efforts were not in vain, that their digging had prolonged the lifespan of the warren and all her structures and institutions. Tom got in his car and drove home. He went up and knocked on the Kurtzes' door. Pam answered.

"Howdy, stranger. How are you? Would you like to come in?"

Tom entered and thanked Pam, told her he'd been out digging, doing his part to protect the warren from its newest foe. Pam sat down on her sofa; she seemed relatively unconcerned by the fire, veering the conversation away from potential tragedy and emphasizing topics relating to leisure and the future.

"Where are you going for a holiday this year, Tom?"

Tom watched her mouth as she spoke; he felt himself getting horny. The constant proximity of death had unleashed a youthful vigor that prompted hard-ons right out of the blue. One night, two weeks before, as Tom sat on her couch, they'd been swept up in the moment. Sandra and Mandy had been asleep, and the conversation had gone back to their younger years, talks of escapades and fornicating had prodded them on. He'd leaned over and kissed her, and they'd fallen into an embrace as each shoved as much clothing off as they could. Pants hung around ankles, and shirts were only partially withdrawn as Tom entered inside of Pam, and the duo partook in a hasty and intense fuck right on the couch. As soon as it was over, Pam had hurried to get dressed, shooed Tom out, told him to come back the next day. When he'd returned, curious of what she had in mind, he'd found her sitting upright and proper on her couch, serving him coffee, explaining that what had happened couldn't happen again. The girls were her priority now. She wanted Tom to understand that they could be friends, amicable neighbors, but nothing beyond that. They would not succumb to the lustful whims of couch sex again. It was a one-off, something to be used as a jump-off in their masturbatory fantasies, nothing more.

"No plans yet," said Tom. "I'm just hoping the whole place doesn't go up in flames before I have the chance."

Pam smiled politely, and Tom stuck his paw in his pocket and shoved his penis to the side.

116

It was Ms. Kenduska to the rescue. She would happily watch the kids as Pam ran out. Pam was relieved; she searched through the closet and found an old gas mask that'd belonged to Jim. She took it and kissed the girls and thanked Ms. Kenduska again. She exited her building and felt the thick smoke enter her lungs; the day had a washed-out feel to it, an orange-brown glow. She put on the mask and walked towards the fire.

She stopped at a pond and looked at herself; she caught her reflection in the ripples of the water and figured that she looked somewhere between an insect and an anteater right now; her nipples stiffened. She walked on as the smoke thickened. She came to a gully; no one was there, and she crossed it and walked forward towards the fire. It didn't take long before she felt the incredible heat, and she looked up and saw a tree house in the midst of being burned. She stood still and watched as the flames ate away at it. She couldn't remember if this was the one that she and Jim had taken refuge in way back when. It was the night Jim had selflessly gone out to rescue her, charged headfirst into danger and then wrapped her up in his arms as they waited out the storm. She watched the tree burn and the ash drift. Her world was restructuring itself again and again and again.

117

Sheriff Huckston had gone down near the fire and parked his patrol car to watch the flames. He still felt disconnected from the whole thing. He turned on the radio.

"That was another zinger for our pals over at Fort Dix... Good news, folks. We hear that rain is on its way tonight. That should dampen the spirits of that darn fire. Police are still asking everyone to stay clear of the zone to the west; markers are up, and detours are in effect. We'll keep you posted if anything changes..."

Sheriff Huckston didn't feel much one way or another concerning the approaching rain clouds. He enjoyed sitting alone out in the forest, surrounded by smoke, diffusing the light, and watching the intricate patterns of flame lick upwards, scratching and pawing—extending itself towards the sky. He wondered what Julie Meyers was up to, how his old receptionist was doing now that she'd set herself up in another warren. He missed her eyes, her face, her tits... He felt the tightening in his core—somewhere below his heart, in the upper regions of his abdomen. Each time he thought of her, this physiological phenomenon occurred. Was this where his love was stored? A precise spot, a tiny sector, that churned at the thought of the most prized and endearing partner? Her shape, her gait, her rhythm and flow, all balancing out to twist at this section and release its flood of emotional information. She was one of the few thoughts that had any effect on him—whether positive or negative—and the sheriff figured that meant something. If the fires were gone by the weekend, he might take a trip to see her. In his mind's eye, he imagined their reunion: the embrace, the pornographic takeover, the final release... He turned up the radio and watched the fire move.

118

Doc had rented a room at the Motel Dion. The accommodations were tight, but Doc could squeeze through, just as he'd been doing lately, and nestle himself inside the cozy room. The rabbits had constructed most of their buildings with added height and width, probably a nod to the rabbits' foresight, as visitors of all shapes and sizes were apt to show up randomly in the warren, requiring shelter or services that the warren seemed more than happy to offer up. Doc found it to be a quaint community with an affable spirit; even in light of all the accumulating trauma he'd heard about and witnessed himself, the rabbits still seemed to continue on their day-to-day cycle without much in the way of griping. He lit a cigarette while seated on his bed and flicked on the TV. The clouds outside had rolled in, and a cooling air mass accompanied their arrival. Doc saw the first drops of rain fall against his window; he walked outside and set his coffee down on the sill, staring up and letting the droplets scatter across his face. The rain picked up, and soon it was falling in sheets.

The fire could not survive such an onslaught, he thought. The random will of the weather gods had saved the warren for another day. Doc raised his mug and toasted the skies.

He stood in his doorway and sipped his coffee, enjoying the newfound coolness, and he watched as a turtle exited the forest and entered the motel's front office, soaked through and through, but keeping its steady-state pace, relaxed and enviably slow. A few minutes later, he emerged from the office and walked his way towards Doc.

"Howdy," said the turtle.

Doc returned the greeting and watched the turtle walk past him and stop at the next motel door.

"Looks like we're neighbors, amigo."

"Yes, sir," said Doc.

"The name's Tyrone."

Doc introduced himself, and he invited Tyrone over for a drink. Tyrone said he had a few things to take care of, but he'd head over in an hour or so, if Doc was obliging. Doc nodded, and the two fellas returned to their quarters as the rain kept up.

119

The TV yelled, "Stagnancy is opportunity yet undeciphered," as Doc topped up Tyrone's glass; the two creatures sat at a small table in Doc's motel room and sipped whiskey.

"So, what's your business here, Tyrone?"

"My cousin's dead. Got killed by that Jack. Thought I owed it to that sombitch to come out here and see what'd happened. Might go visit that family... the, uh..."

"Wentworths?"

"Yeah, them folk. I hear he was with their daughter before he was eaten."

Doc and Tyrone each paused to take a sip. The burn made Doc's face flush.

"Sorry to hear about all that. But the Jack's dead. What good is knowing anything now? There ain't no vengeance in tracking down a dead Jack."

"True enough," said Tyrone. "Something don't feel quite right though, you know? Anyway, it's nice out here. Nice folks, nice fires, nice trees."

Doc looked out the window; it was still raining hard.

"I feel the need to be here is all; Something tells me there's more to this story than everyone's letting on," said Tyrone.

Doc nodded. He looked out in the woods, and he could see a hooded figure in a slicker bobbing and weaving through the trees. He wondered what type of asshole would be out in the rain on such an evening.

120

Tom was wandering around the woods in search of something that he was yet unaware of. He'd been sitting in his apartment, and then, bam! He felt the need to exit the confines of his modestly decorated home. The land was extinguishing itself with the help of the rain; *it was all coming to an end*, he thought. And then he thought about conclusions and denouements as he walked through the forest. Having avoided tragedy time and again, he still couldn't figure out what it all amounted to. He'd survived the assault, but that didn't mean that more weren't coming. Some event was destined to upend him, already in motion somewhere down the line. He wondered about the remaining time (*his* time) as he walked through the forest. The rain had continued its torrential pace, but his slicker was keeping him dry. He looked up and could see no moon. The sky was concave and black. He continued on ahead. He squinted; there was light poking through the trees, a glow emanating from some concealed source. He walked towards it; curious, he climbed a small hill. It was something on the ground, a radiant orb casting off rays. He neared it... a brilliant ball of fur; it moved its feet, and the light began to dim. Tom approached. An unconscious youth, steadily regaining its proper candor, lay in the mud facing the heavens. Tom knelt beside the young rabbit.

"Tilly?"

121

Tim walked up to the girls during recess. Mandy and Sandra were standing near the swing set. They seemed to be involved in some type of serious chat as far as Tim could tell.

"Hey, girls."

Mandy looked up; her initial glance was filled with annoyance and apprehension, but when she realized it was Timothy, her expression morphed, and she beckoned him forward. "What's up, Tim?"

It'd been a strange while, Tim had to admit, but now that the fire had gone out, there seemed to be a sense of calm permeating the air. The sky was cloudless and blue, a cool yet radiant morning in the warren.

Tim couldn't think of anything memorable to say. Since the death of Jack (and particularly after the feast), Tim had felt a strange connection to the Kurtz girls. Their father had killed the beast which had eaten his family, only to succumb to the beast after eating it and thus die at the hands of the very thing he'd killed—yet another victim rounding out its reign of death. *Boy, that Jack was sure a treacherous little prick*, thought Tim. He asked the girls if they'd like to hang out after school. Mandy told him she had soccer practice, and Sandra had homework to finish. Another time, said the girls. They asked him how it was going living with his uncle, and he said, "It is what it is." They all smiled and nodded. The bell rang, and they all walked back to the school's big red doors. Tim poked around in his locker as the other kids re-entered their classrooms. The doors all shut—school resumed—and Tim stayed alone in the hallway; he pushed his straw into his juice box and took a long sip. He sat down feeling comfortably alone. He looked up at the clock in the hallway and watched its hands move.

122

Tyrone was given directions to the Wentworths' home and marched up there the following day. The hike from the motel had been long, but seeing as how lovely the weather was, the journey had been nothing but a darling affair. He smelt the sweetness in the air, the flatulent potpourri of an array of flowers. The mist of the woods. Samantha Wentworth was outside when he got there, playing on the front lawn, a listless cat lying next to her.

"Howdy."

Samantha looked up. "Hey."

"That's a fine-looking cat you got there. You mind if I talk to you for a minute?"

Samantha kept her gaze on Tyrone and shook her head.

Tyrone asked her about Pete and Kristen. He asked whether Kristen had been feeling ill that day, or if she mentioned anything about Pete; he asked how her emotions were: was she calm, noncommittal, irate? Samantha answered matter-of-factly. Tyrone noticed some oddities about the child, somehow simultaneously withdrawn and open in her answers. He figured he wasn't going to get much here, and as he glanced through the window behind her and saw two adult rabbits reclining in the living room—their style immediately evoking a sense of doom and indifference—he figured he wouldn't waste his time or his good humor conversing with their lot. He bid Samantha goodbye and kept on down the road.

When Tyrone got back to the motel, he saw Doc sitting outside his room, sipping on a beer. He offered one to Tyrone who took him up on his offer, and the two gentlemen began to talk again, livening up and resuming where they'd left off the night before. Tyrone told Doc that he'd spoken to the Wentworth girl, but that it'd been a waste of time. They kept drinking, and Tyrone told him that he felt something off in the warren; an oddity existed here that he felt he needed to glimpse or come across. This rambling of words unstuck an idea in Doc's head, and he suddenly felt like showing the Room to Tyrone. He became giddy at the prospect of entering into it again.

"Hey, you wanna see somethin' wild?"

Tyrone smiled, and Doc said, "C'mon, then."

They hurried off, and Doc led the way to Bill's old bunker.

123

When Tom had found Tilly in the woods the night before, he'd thought she might be sick. He'd stared down at her, curious as to how such a young thing could glow in such a manner.

"Are you alright?"

"Tom?" Tilly was coming around. "Yes, I'm fine. Can you help me up?"

Tom took her arm and hoisted the young rabbit to her feet. "You were glowing."

"Oh, yeah?" She didn't seem to care much that such an oddity had occurred. She told Tom to follow her. "I'd like to show you something," she said.

It was strange for Tom, first and foremost, to be wandering around in the rain, prodded on by some nighttime urge to escape his home and venture into the darkness, but then he'd seen the light, little miss Tilly, glowing on the ground, and now he was following her through the woods.

"Where are we going?"

"We're almost there," she said.

Tom looked for markers, designations that might indicate where they'd stepped off to, but suddenly Tom had no clues or navigational know-how. The warren he'd spent his entire life in had simply vanished; trees like he'd never known grew up from the ground. The rain kept up its pace, and Tom attributed its steady stream as the true culprit disorientating and obscuring the land. He heard a growl and paused and looked down at Tilly.

"C'mon," she said. "We're nearly there."

Tom obeyed and continued behind her, purposefully keeping his head bowed, no longer trying to orient himself but following mindlessly, curious of where Tilly was taking him. His tiny tour guide in this misbegotten land.

"Here," she said.

They'd come to a large tree with branches twisting every which way, and Tilly got down and started pulling at a root, and all of a sudden, a portion of the tree's trunk gave way, and a doorway appeared in the center of the tree. Tilly didn't say anything but took his hand and proceeded to climb inside. Tom followed the slanted path downward, and the two rabbits descended deep into the earth.

124

Daybreak, and we're back at the Belting Bird: it's 3 p.m., and customers of all makes and models wander in. It's a time for drink and leisure in the warren, at least to those seated within the bar. Eager bar stars drum their paws against varnished tabletops as barmaids rush around, calming the mood with each beverage placed before its rightful holder.

"Amen," says Mr. Woodhawk as a beer is set down before him.

Sheriff Huckston comes in and sits down at the bar. He orders two shots of whiskey and a pilsner. He takes a shot, then sips at his beer, and orders a pickled egg. Soon he'll be hitting the road. He's taken the next two days off. The plan is in motion: visit Julie Meyers, his ex-receptionist, proclaim his love (or his slightly perverse rendition of it) and see how the cards fall. Will she swoon into his arms? Doubtful, but the sheriff has a growing appetite for the encounter. He feels the need to play out the narrative one way or another. Dixie comes by; she asks if he'd like anything else. The good sheriff declines and tells her he's got to be on his way soon. She smiles and shifts her attention to an old rabbit in the back, hammering away with his hips at the pinball machine. Dixie yells, "Hey, cut it out!" but the old rabbit continues to smash at it in intermittent bursts. Sheriff Huckston turns away and stares at himself in the mirror behind the bar. He smiles and notes the strangeness of his grimace, as if his smile were no longer his, permanently altered and tinged with the perfume of derangement. He takes his last shot of whiskey and exits the Belting Bird.

125

Deputy Dean and Deputy Deidra were back at the station. Deputy Dean grabbed a donut from the main area and refilled his styrofoam cup with coffee. Their shift was set to end in a couple of hours, and they sat around shooting the shit, airing gossip and repeated stories recycled at whim. From everything the day had served up thus far, it seemed like all was well and calm within the warren. The disasters had abated and no longer seemed to threaten the place on such a grand scale: no new monsters, predators, or elemental forces to contend with, only boredom and monotony continued to be a drain. Deputy Dean put a cup on the ground and tossed peanuts at it from his office chair.

"I'm bored," he said.

Deputy Deidra scratched roughly at her clitoral hood. "Maybe some bozo will start another fire or go on some killing spree. Is that what you want?"

Deputy Dean got his next two peanuts in the cup and pumped his paw in the air in a mild-mannered celebration.

"I'm just bored is all."

She understood but didn't want to tell him that. She walked back to the kitchen and looked in the pantry; she closed it and open it, and closed it and opened it again.

126

Pam was at the office. Now that Jean was gone, she'd been promoted to a new position, merging her duties with Jean's responsibilities, and the workload was large. She looked up at the clock on the wall, Jean's old one with its cartoon hands; she had a good twenty minutes left before she had to run out and pick up the girls from school. What would she cook for supper? Did Mandy have soccer tonight? *Shit*, she thought, *she does*. Her phone rang.

"Hello."

"Hi, Pam. It's Gloria Kenduska, your neighbor. You remember that strange fella from down the hall with the weird haircut? George something or other. *He's back*, the bastard"—she trailed off for a moment, mumbling obscenities at the arrival of their long-lost neighbor—"I don't want him here. There's something we must be able to do. A petition. A..."

She kept going, and Pam zoned out. George had departed on some trip months ago, leaving the warren near the beginning of the Jack attacks, missing the entirety of the action, only resurfacing, it seemed, at the close. Rumors of violent confrontations and unlawful activity had surfaced against George in the past, and his demeanor—as Jim had once put it—verged on the reptilian. Pam didn't care one way or another for George and his strange crew cut. In some ways though, she was happy he'd returned. It'd stir the pot just enough to keep Ms. Kenduska from lounging in the main lobby all the time. Pam hated the encounters, the forced chitchat each time she got home.

"I'm sure it'll all work out. I bet George'll just keep to himself, Ms. Kenduska. Don't worry."

"But..."

"I have to go now. Have a great day. Talk soon."

She hung up and took a long breath. She had fifteen minutes left. She scrolled through the never-ending tide of emails. One read, "Beware the Goose." She clicked on it and followed the link. A sea of pop-ups exploded across her screen.

"Fuck!"

She called the extension for computer support. Another virus had infiltrated her system.

"Goddamnit!"

They told her they'd see to it Monday.

127

Tom was lounging at home, blinking dumbly at the TV screen which was currently switched off. Tilly had taken him deep, and he still couldn't wrap his mind around everything she'd shown him. At a certain point, their trek inside the tunnel and the tree had taken them to a hole, a possible outlet into some new frontier.

"Stop here," she'd said. "Now, wait."

He did as she asked—the once-glowing child—and then the tunnel he found himself in began to shake. Tremors jiggled the cave (the tunnel beneath the ancient tree), and he glanced down at Tilly, and she said, "Here she comes."

He watched the black hole in front of him. The upcoming show approaching this large peephole in the earth. It was a texture streaking past, shaking the entirety of the cavern. Scales and puffy flesh. A snake or worm of indefinite proportions on another lap deep beneath the warren.

"Isn't she beautiful?" said Tilly.

Tom didn't know what to think. He watched the circular

hole as the snakeskin drifted by; it continued for minutes on end, vibrating the entire structure.

"It's trying to catch its tail," said Tilly. "It's trying to become the definitive ouroboros."

Tom nodded, having no idea what she meant.

"She controls everything, you see. The master of the Room. Her motions funnel upwards through the earth, communicating up to the fauna and fungi. She trembles the earth and directs its order through her vibrations. She is the unconscious miner prevalent everywhere. The cyclical god trying to devour itself, the energizer bunny at the end of the road."

Tom nodded again, and she said, "This way." She turned him around and walked back up the tunnel and took a hard left fifty or so feet ahead. They could still hear the snake going around and around. They continued along curving terrain until they came to a small door. Tilly grabbed the handle and pushed it open. A great room fell before them. One light flicked on way above, and the immense space disoriented Tom in such a manner that he felt himself growing faint, and he tumbled to his buttocks in order to catch his breath.

"What is this place?"

"It's the Room."

Tom felt his sanity deteriorating; it was all going to hell in a handbasket and mighty quick. He felt the Room spin, the carousel pirouetting above the snake. He felt it grab hold of him, direct his body forward; the Room inspired motion and kicked him out. The next thing he remembered he was above ground—outside of the tree with Tilly. He struggled to his feet, and Tilly said, "I don't think she likes you very much."

128

Doc tossed the door open to Bill's bunker, and Tyrone followed him down the steps. The turtle took his time with the descent, curious about what Doc had to show him—still uncertain of what exactly he was walking into. Doc walked leisurely past all the machinery; the bunker hadn't been touched since the last time he'd entered. It seemed stable within its underground arrangement. Doc walked his way to the tight corridor in the back, and Tyrone followed suit.

"What's this place?"

"An old pal's workstation."

Tyrone grunted and picked up a set of metallic gizmos from the counter. "What's he do?"

"He was a writer," responded Doc. "Now chop-chop, good sir. We're almost there."

They pressed on through the corridor, and Doc warned Tyrone about the narrow enclosure they were entering into and to keep following along.

"The Room's just ahead," he said.

But it wasn't, and the hallway kept going; it narrowed gradually and took unorthodox detours and subtle U-turns.

Where the hell is this thing going? thought Doc.

He didn't want to appear lost to Tyrone, and he tried to put on a confident demeanor. He stressed that they were just a few corners shy of their objective.

Doc muttered, "Fuck," under his breath and kept going; at some point, he ran square into Tyrone, and both fellas seemed to get spun around and muddled as to which direction they were heading to and coming from.

All hope seemed lost.

They walked on for lack of a better plan.

Tyrone was perspiring heavily, and he cursed Doc for his wretched guidance. Then suddenly, they ran smack into it—a door. Doc threw it open. The light blinded them, and each one raised their limbs against the light and walked out from the corridor into the next locale. Doc squinted and looked up. They'd come out of a small rock face, and they were back in the forest again. He saw Tyrone in front of him, staring to the right. Doc turned and saw Jefferson's gas station.

"Hmm," said Doc.

129

Jefferson was watching TV when Doc and Tyrone entered. It'd been a good day so far—bright and lovely out, steady but pleasant inside. He nodded to the pair as they walked the aisles, grabbing their snacks.

"Hey, what's going on with that door out back?" said Doc.

Jefferson scratched his head. "Which door are you talking about, sir?"

"The one in the rock right behind here."

Jefferson wasn't sure what Doc was referring to, so he agreed to follow them out and have a look. The trio exited his shop and curved around the building to where Doc and Tyrone had just exited from. The door was there, and Jefferson had to scratch his head again, saying that he'd never noticed it before. They opened it up and found a small toolshed covered in spiderwebs with an array of hoes and shovels leaning here and there.

Now it was Doc's turn to be confused; he looked at Tyrone who said, "Fuck this place."

Doc stood inside and did a small turn, and he said, "That's not what was here before."

"Things change," said Jefferson. "The nature of today's world."

"I suppose so," said Doc.

He looked at Tyrone who shrugged, just as baffled as before.

Jefferson bid the fellas goodbye and walked back towards the gas station and looked up and hallucinated the clouds forming into a gigantic funnel. *What a show*, he thought.

When he came back into his shop, he saw a strange machine sitting on his counter, right next to the cash register. It had a similar build and bulk. He hit one of the keys and felt something stab at his paw. He pulled it away and saw a tiny drizzle of blood ooze out between the follicles of his fur. He put the typewriter behind the counter, curious how such a machine had suddenly appeared in his shop. He grabbed the newly arrived tabloids and started flicking through them.

130

Tom decided to go for a walk. He had some leftover meat he'd cook up upon his return, and for now, he'd enjoy the day and try to normalize himself, walk a familiar trail, keep all the sights and sounds as banal as he could. The appearance of the snake living deep beneath the warren had brought on ideas of its unseen head bursting through at any point, swallowing the rabbit as he moseyed on dreamily with his day. This would forever haunt him now, or so he thought. Tilly, that little fucker, had shown him the nightmare, and now he was cursed with its knowledge. The being living below them: larger and more violent and powerful in every conceivable sense. What could be done to combat this sickly education? Drink and drugs to numb it, meditation to accept it, suicide to escape it. These were the best options he could come up with. He was still so near the revelation. Inevitably, he hoped, monotony would pave over it, be his kindest friend, his saving grace. He figured that given enough time, and barring any new snake sightings, he'd come to acclimate to the idea of a giant reptile circling their territory and cultivating its own strange modifications and events. So long as the deaths remained predictable (Jacks, fires, poisonings, and disease), he'd be able to resume his life, perhaps slightly altered, but nonetheless continued in more or less the same ordinary fashion.

When he returned to his building, he took the elevator with Ms. Kenduska. He asked her how she was today, and she said, "I gots the cancer, and it's eighty-nine degrees out. How do you think I'm doing, Tom?"

Tom smiled awkwardly, and the elevator doors opened. He stepped out. "Bye, Ms. Kenduska."

She grunted in retort.

131

Tim took a detour after school. He walked towards the
Basquiat Farm and followed it west and found himself in a
region that had been eaten away by the fire. He walked on
through scorched debris. He found an array of animals burnt
up: hedgehogs, deer, squirrels, and mice. He was fascinated
by the destruction that the fire had caused. At school, his
teacher had spoken to them about renewal and the cost of
rebirth and so forth. She had tried to put a positive spin on a
ruthless and chaotic event, to find the narrative that would
appease their anxieties, speak to their sensibilities, and Tim
felt pity for her and the rest of the class. He leaned over the
burnt corpse of an elk and touched it. Oily ash clung to his
paws, and he wiped the debris on his pants. He sat down a
few feet away and looked thoughtfully at the landscape he
found himself in. He wished he was a painter and could
capture the subjective beauty of this place. He didn't realize
it then, but he'd taken the first step in cultivating an idea
that would obsess him for the rest of his days. And as he sat

in the midst of this destroyed world, he had a comforting thought. He realized he didn't need a home anymore, just a very basic and simple Room.

132

A synopsis of what Jefferson wrote during his first shift with the typewriter:

A famous writer, John Laureson, pens his fifth and final book; it is said to be his most outrageous outing yet. Only three copies are made, and a lottery is developed to choose three potential readers. Once chosen, the readers are taken to one of three undisclosed locations around the globe to read the book in utter isolation. Once the book is read, the reader is freed, and each reader converses with a variety of experts and writers and hypnotists to re-create from figments of their imagination, memory, and unconscious a new version of their most recent literary ingestion. The three teams piece together three versions of the same book, and two are deemed lousy, but one is already viewed as a classic. Twenty-five years later, the original is released, and they compare the best version against it. The results are surprising (oscillating between two very different poles), and as it turns half the population mad with envy, the cojones of the writer swell to an unfathomable size as the world prepares to eat him. He stands his ground and waits.

Jefferson was having fun typing away behind the counter. He heard the door open and looked up pleasantly. It was Pam, and he gave her a hearty wave. He saw a flash of revulsion appear across her face; he glanced down and noticed that his paws were covered in blood.

"Ah, man," he said.

"Are you alright?"

"Yeah, must've nicked myself. Nothing to worry about, dear. How's your day going?"

Pam sighed. "It's been a day, all right." She paid for her gas and a small basket of groceries. "Toodle-oo," she said.

133

When Pam got home, Sandra was on the couch plugging away at her homework. Mrs. Dungbry would soon be dropping Mandy off after practice. Pam preheated the oven and went to work prepping the supper for herself and the girls.

"Mom!" yelled Sandra.

"Yes?"

"What are we having?"

"Chicken, and don't yell. If you want to talk to me, come into the kitchen."

She heard Sandra slunk off the couch and come her way.

"Mom, I need help with my homework."

"No problem. After I get supper on, we'll take a look, okay?"

Sandra nodded, and they heard a knock at the door. Sandra rushed for it; it was Mandy. Sandra let out a groan.

"Oh, it's you," she said.

"How was practice?"

"Good, Mom. What's for supper?"

Once the food was put away and the dishes cleared, the trio played a game of Hangman's Gin. They laughed and taunted one another, and soon the day was falling away. Pam put the girls to bed, and then she sat on the sofa and poured herself a glass of wine. The television showed her the lavish lives of rich suburbanites with flamboyant personas. She watched it to fill the evening void.

134

It was an exciting day. The radio announced the arrival of the perennial ball. This was a big to-do in the warren, demarking the end of one cycle and the beginning of another. They would all dress up, fashion their best costumes, and come dolled up to the nines. The voice of Pete van Everdynk said: *"All right, dear listeners. The word is out. Next Friday is the baronial ball.* La soirée des masques, *the monster mash, the absolute evening we've all been waiting for. Grandparents, runts, genitors, and siblings—come one, come all. 7 p.m. at St. Joe's School. Doors open at 6 p.m."*

The girls could hardly contain themselves. The ball was all they could talk about as the week flew by. Pam had a hard time getting them to mention anything else. They discussed their costumes and the possible announcements that might surface at the ball. They giggled in the back seat as Pam drove them to school. Everyone seemed to be in a brighter mood. The excitement even extended to Ms. Kenduska, who winked at Pam in the hallway and told her she had a special treat planned for the evening.

Tom was gearing up too. Although he hadn't been seen much over the last week, he was using the celebration as a means of clearing his mind. A tool to focus on. He rummaged through his closet and concocted his ensemble. He found scarfs and fabric and cut and pulled and sewed. He dove right in and worked like a maniac to give his mind solace from the monster below. He hadn't seen Tilly since that night and had no interest in crossing paths with her again. She knew things he didn't wish to understand, so he bore down and concentrated on the task at hand. He crafted his costume in the darkness of his apartment. Thick bags hung around his eyes as he cut maniacally around the fringes of his newfound getup.

Doc and Tyrone were told about the ball by the receptionist of the motel, and they decided to have a look. They were asked to come as anything but themselves. They were to unbind their faces and reveal the masks below. "Aces," said Doc, and Tyrone got into the spirit too. They sat outside their rooms most nights, eyeing the night sky and sipping on suds.

Over the coming week, Tim and Curtis planned out their attire and had a good time preparing for the festivities in their burrow. And the deputies sang and worked on ideas at the station between calls of domestic abuse and roadkill cleanup.

Jefferson barely paid attention to any of it. He played the keys on his new typewriter and fell into a rhythm that was antagonistic to the one currently rippling through the warren. His mind had latched on to a tidal wave of words, rushing forth in ghastly sentences.

135

Sheriff Huckston had stayed in a motel just outside of Julie Meyers' warren near Lymburn for the better part of a week now. He was wild and ragged-looking. He seemed to have gained in bulk and size. He ate at the diner across the street and filled up on munchies from the vending machine. He kept the "Do Not Disturb" sign on his door. His room smelt of sweat and semen. He didn't shower and kept the TV on all day and all night even though he barely watched it. He knew why he'd come—to see Julie—but somehow that errand or goal seemed futile now. And as each day passed, he seemed less and less inclined to go through with it. The proximity of his goal (Julie being but a ten-minute drive away) seemed to somehow make it all the more impossible to accomplish; he'd been halted at the finish line. *Rats*, he thought. To have come so far, to be so close, and yet be undone by nothing at all right at the bitter end. He blamed his endocrine system, the rebelling glands of his being. To be thwarted by your insides in such a manner seemed on par with what the sheriff had come to expect from the world at this point. *It is what it is*, thought Sheriff Huckston, and he walked out to the front office and paid for another night before returning to the vending machine for much-needed supplies.

289

136

It's Thursday, and the rabbits are attending to last-minute details. The school's staff along with a self-appointed committee of volunteers are decorating the St. Joe's gymnasium. Tables are set up in a row, lined together to bear the weight of the beverages and finger foods that are to adorn them the following night. The stage is set for multiple modes as a play, a band, and a special announcement are currently in the works. Mrs. Banderas will don the role of DJ, her chosen handle being DJ Polymorphous. Pam is there, helping wrap the place in decorative cloth and other ornamentation. Ms. Kenduska came with her and has agreed to help—although she's currently sitting in a chair, barking orders at the younger teaching staff, telling them how to properly calibrate the lighting, her preferred ambience being dimly lit, with candles accenting the tables near the edges of the room, and punctuated by random bursts from two high-powered strobe lights nestled to the left and right of the main stage. The staff are trying to ignore her recommendations to no avail.

"No, not that one. Push the button to the left! Dim it more, goddamnit!"

Mr. Headwick is moments away from telling Ms. Kenduska to shove it up her ass. He storms out of the gymnasium and lights a cigarette before he's even exited the building. The brisk air calms him as he takes deep inhales. His lungs pull in air and carcinogens, and he feels happy at the fact that he's alive. The sky is dark grey, and the clouds have a vertical feel, elongating the depth of the sky as it hangs precariously above. He blows smoke at them, and it drifts and disintegrates a few feet away. He takes a few final breaths and goes back inside to face the old spinster in the gymnasium, revitalized by the reprieve of the cigarette in the school playground.

Pam smiles at him as he re-enters the gym. The place is coming together. Pam thinks it'll be another success. She can't wait for the girls to see it. Pete van Everdynk is setting up his station to broadcast live from a booth in the corner. He'll highlight the event for those sitting at home or driving along (he says, "Test... test..." into his microphone), keeping everyone informed of the social hubbub occurring at tomorrow night's ball. The theme seems to be traditional, and the decorations hark back to the balls of old. Stick figurines adorn most tables, incorporated into their centerpieces, and drawings of rabbits dancing around the fire in plain beige dress are recurring motifs on many tablecloths. And then DJ Polymorphous plays a tune, and a technologically savvy student adjusts the lights—green, blue, and red beams move about the stage and dance floor in oblong shapes, and it is obvious to everyone that times have changed. Ms. Kenduska shouts, "Where's the strobe light?" And the student flicks a switch, and Marny, a teacher's aide, falls into an epileptic fit.

The house lights come on, and everyone circles around her. Deputy Dean agrees to take her to the hospital once she comes around. The others stay and continue to prep. The ball is almost ready. The party will soon begin.

137

Jefferson was in a sweat. He was typing away at another short story, so eager to understand its motions and movements that his brain was simultaneously open and closed to what it was doing. And as he tried to think about what was going to happen, his fingers beat him to the punch and resolved his issue or created an altogether new one to follow along with, thus blazing new roads to new pastures and expanding the narrative thread. But he was still an anxious mess. This mode operated above him: he couldn't control it. It just happened of its own accord. When would it come to an end? How would it halt? Would it leave him just as quickly as it first appeared? Or perhaps it was here to stay? A permanent fixture?

So much goddamn uncertainty.

He read what he'd written and felt a strange sense of relief fall over him. *It was going to be okay,* he thought. He stared up from behind the cash register at his gas station and found it dark and unpopulated. The lights seemed to dim suddenly; flagrant blackness surrounded him. *What the hell?* he thought.

He heard a young girl's voice, the swinging of a teeter-totter. The place had abruptly shifted, and this new arena seemed much larger, eating up his little gas station within its grand design. He heard the rushing of water, an aggressive outflow coming his way, and then the Room faded, and he was back where he belonged, behind the counter. He shook his head, and his one ear flopped around from side to side. He popped a Percodan from his stash and ate a hotdog and chalked the whole thing up to another strange occurrence in a strange world. He flipped the sign on the door and closed up shop, and then he went back to the typewriter and continued to work.

138

Sheriff Huckston woke up suddenly. There was a splitting pain in his guts. He rolled out of bed, gripping his stomach, and hustled to the bathroom. The moment he sat down, it all came loose, and he shook in pleasure at having made it just in time. He banged his fist against the wall and wiped his ass. And as he pulled up his drawers and stood in front of the mirror, he stared into his eyes and found that his face looked different. He'd grown a snout. It was strange, a rabbit with a snout—but that's what it was. It had occurred aggressively. Overnight, it seemed. He put his paws against it, raised his lips, and checked out his new teeth.

He felt weird. He'd have to go out tomorrow; he was already getting hungry. But then the others would see what he'd become. This... thing. *Fuck it*, there wasn't any other way. He would adapt to their looks, dance around their pitying gazes, glare straight against their ridicule—if he was hungry enough, nothing else would ever matter. It was a question of insanity and will. Two powers feeding the biological wheelhouse.

He went back to bed and fell sound asleep.
Softly, he mouthed, *"So verrryy hungry."*

139

Pam was having strange dreams (Jim, Bill, Hymen, Jean, you name it... all the past characters of the warren seemed to be cropping up that night, the dead paying her a customary visit). She woke up with tears spilling down her face, her pillow wet from the outburst. She walked to the kitchen and grabbed a glass of water. She stood alone in the dark and looked out her window at the forest. She felt nostalgic and missed her husband. She sat down on the floor for a minute, and then she got up and went to check on the girls. *Tomorrow will be a big day*, she thought. *The girls will be so excited.*

She turned her pillow over and lay with her eyes open, trying to kick-start her mind in some direction—but it just seemed to float in a mood, one mixed with melancholy, and for a time, she gave up and stewed in the strength of the feeling. Images of Jim flashed through her mind, and eventually the pull of sleep took hold without her knowing. When she woke up, the girls were already out in the living room watching TV.

"Good morning, did you already pack your lunches?"

"Uh-huh," said Mandy.

Pam walked over and kissed them each on the head. "Okay, well, go get ready then. I'll drop you girls off at school."

Mandy and Sandra were slow to rise from the floor.

"What time are we going to the ball at, Mom?"

"How does 6:30 sound?"

140

Tom was trying on his outfit. He'd fashioned what he thought might be a conventional robe, but in his ecstasy and craftsmanship, he'd created a flowing gown with an extensive collar design, pinched fabric ran in circular tufts around his neck, and his head popped out from the center. His chapeau was reminiscent of a warrior's mask, covering half his face and curling upwards at the sides like minuscule horns. He looked elegant and strong and slightly evil. He heard a knock at his door. It was George, his long-lost neighbor.

"Hey, George."

George stared blankly at him, taking in the sight of Tom in his gown. "Quite a getup you got there."

"It's for the ball."

"I figured as much." George ran his paw across the top of his head, ruffling his distinctive crew cut which immediately resumed its former rigidity. "Listen, have you seen this petition Ms. Kenduska is circulating?"

Tom shook his head.

"That bitch is trying to get me thrown out"—he mumbled a few expletives—"if it comes your way, let me know, okay? I really don't have time for this shit."

He walked away without another word. He was hunched over as he moved, growling to himself; he punched a door open and disappeared from the corridor.

Tom was left standing in his doorway; his helmet drooped down, and he figured he'd add a bit more stuffing to the inside of it, making it a snugger and comfier fit. He went back inside and stared at himself in the mirror. He made a coquettish face and then an evil one. He walked over to the fridge and cracked a beer and sat down at the kitchen table all prim and proper like.

141

Tim was putting on a hat that he and Curtis had fashioned over the week. It had golden beads clasped together, forming its shell, and a large horn sticking out from its top. Curtis had donned a mask he'd concocted from old Halloween costumes, stitching two or three latex coverings to craft his newly minted one. Whereas Tim's costume held a certain level of grace, Curtis appealed to a more guttural, DIY approach. Having been to prior balls a time or two before, Curtis knew that this ragtag methodology of design was as popular as the courtly one. He and Tim would each blend in seamlessly with the crowd. Curtis poured himself a glass of wine and then walked over to the kitchen and grabbed a small glass; he poured a few ounces into it and handed it to Tim.

"Drink up," he said. "It's good for the bones, and it'll get your dancing feet in high order for this evenin'."

Tim thanked his uncle and took a sip. They sat down on the couch and talked about their world before Curtis glanced down at his watch and said, "It's about time we get this show on the road. What do ya think?"

Tim nodded, and the duo moseyed out of their burrow towards Uncle Curtis' SUV.

142

Doc and Tyrone arrived shortly after 6:15 p.m. They'd been sampling some alcoholic concoction from Doc's flask while wandering through the woods. There were spotlights set up outside the school, whirling around all across the night sky in a multitude of colors. Doc had noticed them during their stroll and supposed the rabbits had gone all out for the event.

In the end, Doc had untethered his face; he'd pulled off his human mask, unwrapped the barbwire and removed all bits of the fowl disguise. When he'd stared at himself in the mirror, the final configuration of his face made him wince. He was ugly and ripped and broken like a tortured convict limp on the cross, puffed up and red. When he'd shown Tyrone (who'd opted for a more traditional suit and tie configuration), he'd said that Doc's look would certainly turn some heads. He left it at that, and after a few beers out front on the motel's veranda, the duo set off to the ball, ready to partake in a sumptuous night of excessive shenanigans.

As they entered the school, they were met by Ms. Kenduska sitting at the entrance table. She scowled at Doc and told them that donations were mandatory. Tyrone and Doc each popped a five-dollar bill into the jar that said "For Community Affairs" on it. Ms. Kenduska grunted at them as they entered the gymnasium.

Pam wandered over and was the first to greet them. Her smile widened even as she took in the horror of Doc's face and welcomed the two gentlemen to the ball. She told them to sit wherever they liked and to help themselves to the food and beverages. Doc thanked her and watched as she made her way through the crowd, shaking paws with an assortment of folks.

It was already quite packed, and Doc and Tyrone found a seat close to the wall at a table with an electrician, a doctor, and Mr. Woodhawk. They introduced themselves before going up to the bar and grabbing a scotch and a tequila chaser. They clinked glasses and took a drink and turned their attention to the dance floor. A large rabbit in a flowery muumuu performed her jig, and as the music faded into the next song, Tyrone heard the gasping lungs of the obese rabbit war against the depletion of her airflow as she succumbed to a folding chair to recuperate with a noticeable thump.

143

Sheriff Huckston raged against the machine. He'd eaten his way through eight full-size meals at the diner including the fish and chips, hamburger deluxe, mac and cheese, and the goat stew. He'd fallen asleep ungracefully on the toilet not long after returning to his room. The sun shined through on the comatose glutton from the bathroom window; he burped, unconscious, and dreamt of Jean Pomagrowski.

And she said this: "You either follow the Self or the Words. These are the only two perspectives. The Self wants to see itself succeed, wants to win, wants the power. The Words want to transgress the Self and discover the tone under-lining the beast, assess the reason why it does what it does, the Words reaffirming the animal. Restructuring the ghost inside."

The sheriff woke up with a start. There was drool seeping down his snout; he farted and waddled over to the bed. The restaurant staff had looked on at him in disgust that day, and he'd grown so large in his belly that three or four of his shirt buttons remained undone—no longer able to cover his furry underside. But he didn't care; the insatiable hunger had blotted out all manner of distractions. It had given him perfect focus directed at a simple goal. He fell back asleep almost instantly. His body was breaking down in a variety of ways, seeking to transform his anatomy to match his newfound will. The hunger had rerouted him and remained his only steadfast state. He was becoming an immaculate eating mechanism.

And the church bells rang in the nearby warren, and the sheriff heard none of it.

144

Tom arrived at the ball shortly after 7 p.m. slightly nervous as he extricated himself from his vehicle. He waved to the Booramites, a couple of rabbits clasping hands; the man wore a top hat and monocle, whereas the madam wore a witchy mask with an elongated nose and a simple lace dress. Mr. Booramite tipped his hat as he and his wife walked across the darkened lawn towards the school's red doors.

Tom stumbled his way up, careful to keep his gown from dragging on the asphalt path; he held the sides as he made his way to the entrance.

Upon entering, he saw Ms. Kenduska. Her look betrayed her disapproval at his getup. Tom felt more nervous than ever. He felt a mild tremor run through the floor, and a brief image of the snake flashed through his brain. He walked up to her table and plopped a few coins in the donation bucket; neither rabbit said a word.

It was Mandy who first came running up to him. She welcomed him with a big hug.

"How's it going, little lady?"

"I'm having such a wonderful time, Tom. Isn't it beautiful here?"

Tom smiled and nodded. "Is your mom about?"

Mandy turned and pointed to Pam, elegantly dressed and coronated with a crown of ribbons and thorny roses, talking to Sally Hearse near the punch bowl.

He smiled and pivoted his gaze and saw Suzette to his left. She came up to him holding the hand of another rabbit dressed in a tux with a black blindfold and only one eyehole cut into it.

"Tom, you look wonderful. This is my boyfriend, Drew."

Tom shook the rabbit's paw; Drew said nothing and firmly gripped Tom's mitt, inducing a small convulsion of pain.

"Well, it was nice seeing you; enjoy your evening, Tom."

Tom watched the couple wander off as Suzette laughed and snickered with her boyfriend.

Tom surveyed the scene as he unconsciously stretched out his paw. He watched the younglings zigzag their way through the dance floor, laughing and yelling, mixed up in the playfulness and noise of the evening.

The music faded away, and Mrs. Banderas took the stage and announced the upcoming entertainment: a play performed and written by the little ones. Many rabbits went back to their seats, while Tom tucked himself closer to the wall as he focused his attention on the stage. The curtains opened, and Tom watched as a young male rabbit said: "Oh, gosh! Oh, jeez! I think I'm lost. Oh where, oh where might I be!?"

A little thing in a white onesie appeared onstage.

"Little rabbit, little rabbit, are you a lone, wandering whelp? I am the enchantress of Pearl B. Forest. Come, come, let me help..."

Tom squinted and noticed Tilly—the actor—performing her lines in the white garb—the tiny sorceress. He shuttered and felt his stomach churn. He decided to step out for a minute. He cautiously moved his way through the crowd and out into the hallway near the back. Only a few lights remained on, and the hallway was dark and mysterious. He took a sip of water from the fountain and saw George posted up against the wall.

"Hey, George. Taking a breather?"

George nodded.

Tom had the feeling he wanted to be left alone, so he went in the opposite direction. He checked out his old school and walked past the library. He pressed his nose against the glass and felt the rush of forgotten memories crush his being; it was a warm wave of nostalgia breaking him down. He smiled and kept on and returned to the main entranceway through the hallways. Ms. Kenduska passed him in the opposite direction. He smiled at her, and this time, she smiled back.

145

"So, what is it?"

Ms. Kenduska couldn't hide her disgust, but moments later, her lip curled, and she smiled at George. "I have an offer for you, George."

"Okay."

"I don't like you, and you don't like me. There, it's been said. But I don't want to go dragging this damn thing out any longer than I have to. I'm an old rabbit, and the time I got left ain't much. How about we put this thing to bed? You keep your business outside the building and away from me, and I'll stop with this petitioning nonsense."

George eyed her up and down and coughed up a big loogie. He spat it out on the school floor. "Fuck you, you old bitch."

Ms. Kenduska's smile widened. "Have it your way, George."

She turned and walked back to the gymnasium. George felt his phone vibrate. An unknown number had just sent him the location for a pickup. They were early; it wasn't supposed to be until later on that night. Anyway, it wasn't far, a five-minute walk. So he exited the school and took the route through the woods. The night was clear and the moon full. It was easy to navigate, and his phone tracked the package to a box set up on a stump near a large deciduous tree. The box was long and rectangular and red with gold stars adorning its outside. George reached inside and felt around for the handle. He tried to turn it, but it wouldn't budge, and then— slice! He screamed and pulled his arm out. His entire paw was missing, and blood shot out and flowed in an array of directions from his newfound stump; George could only remain conscious for a few brief seconds before he slumped over and passed out. His crew cut remained rigid and un- changed as a spider walked nimbly up the side of his head.

Ms. Kenduska sat outside the gymnasium near the do- nation bin; she put her phone back in her bag and pushed the metallic glove with its sharp, scissor-like fingers to the side, nicking her paw ever so slightly as she withdrew it and sucked up the small droplet of blood.

146

Deputy Dean was on duty. He was there to keep the peace and stick to the sidelines, only venturing in if the shenanigans exceeded far beyond the general, acceptable dose. He stood in the corner of the gymnasium drinking some punch and watching the band perform onstage. He was tapping his foot to the beat as best he could and wearing a goofy grin as he bobbed about; his holstered gun jiggled along with his unfocused dance moves. He wished he could have dressed up for the ball, but a young deputy had called in sick at the last minute, and Deputy Dean had agreed to take his post.

He had discussed some doozy combinations with Deputy Deidra: a black blazer with a cream-colored undershirt and a spiraling armadillo hat. He'd planned to wear sunglasses and a cravat to add further dimensions to the outfit, but the ensemble would have to wait—work required his attention.

Deputy Deidra, meanwhile, was dancing, swaying her hips and pumping away to a cover of "Pablo Picasso." She'd always loved that tune.

She was quite drunk but mostly orderly, and she wore a white wedding dress and a girthy circle of lipstick around her mouth. She powered her way through the song, and Deputy Dean watched her as she danced with her eyes closed. *She seems to be having fun*, he thought.

Curtis and Tim were dancing too. Tim's horn bounced around, and Curtis had a loose circle of friends jittering along to the melody around them. He kept smiling as he stole glances at Tim, who seemed to come alive under the spell of the music. The young rabbit was in a trance of happy convulsions, and Curtis felt the rush of tears momentarily sting his eyeballs. He blinked them away and kept dancing. He looked at the mural on the wall: it was Bernard the Bear, the St. Joe's mascot. He used to dream about it when he was in school. He'd see it running through the woods, rode by a man with a feline face, bearing a snake in one hand and a trumpet in the other. He'd seen this entity many times when he was a kid. He supposed its origin dated back to some magical mix of unconscious chemistry, these large-scale illustrations mixed with an array of neural devilry. He remembered it riding gracefully through the woods, a pale-blue overture as it bulldozed its way through his mind. He looked up and saw a person with a really fucked-up face; he tried to smile at him, but Doc kept on without so much as a gander in his direction.

147

Doc had the feeling that it was time to go—not from the ball (in fact, Doc was having a marvelous time) but from the warren itself. He wasn't sure how he knew that his time was up here, but it was... Tomorrow he'd head out, follow his feet and intuition elsewhere, see where the goddamn road decided to take him. He felt good and calm about it. That was important. He'd let Tyrone know, perhaps they'd even strike out together. But tonight, he'd enjoy the festivities and surrender to the collective chaos. His face felt good being out in the open—vulnerable and hideous. And somehow, he knew life was going to be good for a while. That was a promising sentiment. He walked up to his table holding an armful of drinks; he handed one to Tyrone and two to Mr. Woodhawk and the doctor apiece. He set the last one down in front of his seat, and he sat and watched Tom dance in his wild and captivating costume. He hoped he'd be able to talk with him later on. His style interested Doc—or at least it did in his slightly drunken state. He tipped back the last of his drink and told his tablemates that he had to pee. He walked off slowly, comfortably fading into the party, at one with the saccharine sweetness of a cozy and mature transition.

All the while, Tom kept dancing; the booze had provided the impetus to get him out there and shake his tail; and now, in peak form, he whirled around, his gown flowing effortlessly against the strobe lights. Stops and starts of tripping the light fantastic. Pam nudged up beside him and grazed his trapezius. Tom spun around and wore a big grin; his horned helmet remained firmly in place. She let out a raucous laugh, and Tom paused, momentarily stunned by her beauty. They danced together, and Tom really wanted to kiss her.

In the bathroom, Doc stared at himself in the mirror. Someone had etched into it, "Everyone needs a church." The warm breeze of the evening was making its way in through an open window, and an owl let out a tu-whit tu-whoo. Doc looked into his eyes and wondered about the health of his retinas... and then he hoped he'd get his trumpet blown that night—but he doubted that outcome very much.

148

Jefferson wrote happily in his gas station and giggled at his progress. He was proud of himself for having made it to this new frontier. He looked around the gas station and was exultant about his fecund little space. He was getting used to the constant pricks of the machine, accepting the sacrifice that went along with the work. Sally-Joe Buford popped into his head for some reason, and he thought of her and what she might have been like if she hadn't been eaten all those years ago. Adult Sally-Joe, dissociated from the Jack, reclaiming her name, her brand, and rewriting the history of it all. Her ending had concluded on a vicious note, making her a celebrity victim, a cautionary tale told throughout the warren. He wondered what she might think of her close association with her killer. He imagined her in the psychosphere of the warren, forever stuck in its small intestine, her story's final resting place. In some ways, he hoped to dislodge her from there. Craft a new tale that might shake the established order and move all that shit along. Design a new sequence for her, dress her up in words, and force the digested bits out the warren's asshole, freeing up space, offering solace to the old horrors and room to process the new ones. The healing power of a well-structured fiction. He checked his watch and figured he still had time to go to the ball. He rummaged through the lost and found, searching for a suitable costume, and he found a chimp mask lying near the bottom of the box. He scooped it up and placed it over his head. It would certainly do for his purposes. He locked up his shop and started out towards the school.

149

The sheriff woke up with a start. His stomach roared, and he keeled over in the fetal position in the bed. He was suddenly aware of how large he'd gotten. Even all tucked up, he was the size of the damn mattress. "*So verrryy hungry,*" he said. Sheriff Huckston climbed to his feet and squeezed out the motel door. It was a clear night, and he pushed on into the forest. The diner was closed, and he needed something substantial, something more than vending machine goodies. What could he eat? Who could he devour? He heard a noise coming from up ahead. He lifted his snout into the air and sniffed. The scent he caught aggravated his already agitated hunger. He walked towards it. He moved a bush out of the way and saw a small rabbit. Suddenly this little creature had become the antidote to his ailment, the panacea for his insatiable appetite. He approached, salivating aggressively and smacking his lips. The young rabbit turned and caught sight of him. She screamed and started to run. Instantly, as if by impulse, the sheriff ran after her. *So verrryy hungry,* he thought. He was gaining on her, ready to snatch her up in his jaws, chew up her fat, grind her bones, munch her muscles into mush. They went through a clearing, and Sheriff Huckston saw the approaching road. He ran with all his might, almost there. A few feet away—he lunged and she ducked and he flew by her and onto the road. He saw the lights. The orbs. A screech, a horn, and the unmistakable sensation of being blown apart.

The truck came to a halt some thirty feet away. Peter B. Wells got out, shaken and in awe of what he'd just clobbered with his truck. Suzanne Harper came out from the woods panting.

"Are you okay?" asked Peter.

Suzanne nodded, staring at the broken carcass of Sheriff Huckston smeared up and down the roadway. "He was chasing me," she said.

"It's all right now, little one. Just take it easy, alright?"

Suzanne sat on the side of the road as Peter made a call. She watched as one of Sheriff Huckston's hooves convulsed, some late-game impulse as the animal shut down and ceased to be.

A family drove by in a van, and the little boy in the back seat stared out the window. It was the first time he'd encountered this type of unraveling. The imagery in the headlights... and he burped; his father asked if he needed anything. And the boy shook his head, and his father accelerated the van and picked up speed. The boy turned and looked out the back window. There had been no point in stopping. There was nothing they could do for them now.

150

The ball was reaching its climactic moment. Most of the adults were somewhat inebriated, and the little ones were hopped up on sugar. Ms. Kenduska had joined the party and was dancing near Pam and Tom and the girls. Pete van Everdynk was dismantling his station; he'd been broadcasting most of the night. Now it was time for him to join the fiesta. The dance floor was in a flurry of cycles, spirals, and loops. Jefferson entered the gymnasium. His mask obscured a portion of his vision and made it difficult to breathe—but he was still happy to have it. The music came to a slow halt, and Maureen Redhorn took the stage accompanied by Mr. Headwick. They approached the microphone, and Mr. Headwick said, "Alright, everyone, we'd like to make a big announcement. Maureen Redhorn, our town elder, has informed me that she is retiring from her role, and as such, a new elder must be crowned. She's written the name of the rabbit who will soon fill this role on this little scrap of paper. If you all give me your attention for a brief moment, I'd like to read it to you."

Maureen beamed at the audience and turned her head. Mr. Headwick unfolded the paper as everyone stood watching him.

"Tilly Thursberg, would you please come up to the stage."

Tom spit out a mouthful of his rum and Coke.

Tilly walked casually up to the stage. She shook hands with Mr. Headwick, and Maureen Redhorn gave her a big hug. She took the microphone.

"It is an honor to be called upon for this role," she said. "I feel anxious and excited to step into it. Ms. Redhorn has been such a wonderful and wise elder; I only hope to do her justice and serve the warren well."

Maureen walked to the side of the stage and grabbed a small terrarium. A Pacman frog was inside the glass container. She set it down on a stool in the middle of the stage; someone handed her a paper bag, and she opened the top of the terrarium and emptied the bag inside. A giant maggot fell into it. The frog remained still as the maggot thrashed about.

Mr. Headwick asked Tilly if she had any advice for the warren.

And she said, "No one knows why we are here. The best lives are usually emboldened and structured around doing some task, some vocation. I have little advice and few opinions. But inevitably—or so it seems—the best of us aspire to nothing. Such monumental ambition is often beyond the scope of even the most hardened souls."

Jefferson's paws started to bleed.

"And remember, I ain't your enemy, but I ain't your friend either. And I plan on dying very sloppily, riffing on platitudes in the eye of the hurricane." The crowd remained hushed, and they all bowed down to her standing before them. And she let out her great 'n' barbaric yawp.

Her philosophy was simple: keep it interesting, no matter the cost.

And the Pacman frog and maggot tussled onstage. The frog had the giant bastard halfway in its mouth as Tilly stood there, and the crowd stared up at their tiny new elder.

And so it was: she was their country and western superstar in the best sense of the word, trying to work out interesting ways to get to yet another cliché. She was striving to understand the laziness at the heart of ambition—that so much was achieved based on what you didn't do, how backwards it all was. She smiled vaguely at them, and in her grimace was the pain and understanding of one finally pulling into focus the exquisite details of their journey. The true reflection of her own personal hell. It was a shock to witness young Tilly under this new light, determined to bring herself to the top spot, no matter the cost. She bit her tongue and drew blood and spit it all out on the ground. Someone clapped, and that was it.

That's how it ends.

The carnival of animals, or the danse macabre.

Amen, sister.